C000110932

THE QUIET SPACE BETWEEN US

N.A. COOPER

BLOODHOUND
— BOOKS —

Copyright © 2023 N.A. Cooper

The right of N.A. Cooper to be identified as the Author of the Work has been
asserted by her in accordance with the Copyright, Designs and Patents Act 1988.

First published in 2023 by Bloodhound Books.

Apart from any use permitted under UK copyright law, this publication may only
be reproduced, stored, or transmitted, in any form, or by any means, with prior
permission in writing of the publisher or, in the case of reprographic production,
in accordance with the terms of licences issued by the Copyright Licensing
Agency.
All characters in this publication are fictitious and any resemblance to real
persons, living or dead, is purely coincidental.

www.bloodhoundbooks.com

Print ISBN: 978-1-5040-8343-0

ALSO BY N.A. COOPER

Ripple Effect

Unravelling Alice

For my husband

CHAPTER ONE

I t was early morning – too early for the birdsong she usually woke to. The silence blew towards her off the land, coming from places she couldn't recall. She could see her breath turn to mist in front of her, suspended in the cool air that surrounded the meadows. She stretched her back and yawned, twisting to one side and then the other until she heard the gentle crack she'd been searching for.

She'd woke early to see the Pink Moon – the full moon for April – which sat bright and low in the sky, almost touching the horizon. It was named after the moss-pink phlox which indicated the beginning of spring, but this morning it was the simple milky white she was used to and she couldn't help but feel cheated. It anchored her, the moon, to the month and the passing of time. It hadn't always been that way, but there was so little left for her to cling on to now.

She sat cradling a mug of camomile tea on the uneven doorstep of the house, looking out across the fields. There was a light dusting of frost clinging to the grass which, when illuminated by the watery moonlight, looked quite beautiful but not at all like spring. She was aching for the long winter to pass;

the cold somehow accentuated her loneliness, especially in a place like this. It made the empty spaces feel even emptier, harsher, bereft of any comfort or warmth to ease her pain.

She pulled her robe closed tighter across her chest and brought her mug to her lips, enjoying the warmth of the steam on her face before she drank. Somewhere in the distance she could hear a long, shrill screaming sound – far away at first then growing steadily closer until it was directly above her. A barn owl looking for prey, its wings spread wide, gliding on a light breeze.

Ida remembered the first time she'd heard the high-pitched screeching sound – she'd panicked, thinking someone was coming. As far as she was concerned, owls hooted and people screamed. She'd stood on the little stoop with a pair of binoculars in the hazy light of the dawn, pointing them first across the fields and then up into the trees which stood on the other side of the dip. It had sat in one of the sycamores for quite some time, allowing her to get a good look at it until, spotting something Ida wasn't able to see, it dived to catch its dinner.

It had taken her heart a while to calm and she'd swiftly added it to the list of sounds she kept in a notebook by her bed, joining the howling noise of the wind when it blew through the hills, the barks and howls of the foxes and the bleats and grunts of the wild deer – to name a few. When she heard something that panicked her and her brain refused to think logically, she would find comfort in her list because the sounds she heard were almost always on there. The edges of the paper were curled now and some of the writing was disturbed by creases, but it was still there – comforting in black and white. It had been a while since she'd added anything new.

There were few surprises after so many years, but one thing that continued to amaze her was the power of her imagination – in the worst imaginable way. It's a cruel and brutal thing to experience, being unable to trust yourself and your judgement. Sometimes, even when she knew something to be true, even when faced with indisputable evidence that it was just a bat or a rabbit, a fox or a rat, she managed to catastrophise and spiral until she could no longer be sure about anything. She didn't trust herself, that was the simple truth of it, and the one person she *did* trust was hardly ever here – not that she could blame him for that.

It had always seemed remarkably unfair to Ida that she was forced to spend so much time by herself – her own worst critic. Her mind was her keeper, it had stopped her from doing so many things while forcing her to do others. She didn't fight it anymore, there was no point, she just accepted that it would always be that way. But that didn't stop her from yearning for company while simultaneously hoping it never arrived.

She looked out over the fields of green in front of her – wild and untamed – which led to the rolling hills miles to the north. To the left of her was the river which ran through the dip in the land and, beyond that, the edge of the forest, so thick and dense she could barely see through the treeline. She wasn't a prisoner here, she told herself; how could she ever think that when there were lakes in her back garden and mountains on her doorstep. The clean air of the Welsh countryside was a privilege; she breathed it in, the earthy scents so familiar but never taken for granted.

The shrill cries of the owl disappeared as the moon sunk below the horizon, pulling the light of the sun which steadily transformed the landscape, edging closer and closer until it bathed Ida's face in a warmth that had long since left her tea. She watched as her shadow appeared at an angle beside her, short and skewed, and as the frost melted away from the meadows revealing new life underneath, a chaotic mix of wilderness grappling for a taste of spring.

Still Ida sat there, watching as the night turned to day and trying to identify the exact moment it happened. Of course, she couldn't see the precise second the change occurred, as with many things it was more of a process than something sudden and instantaneous; much like how she ended up here alone.

CHAPTER TWO

She planned to start sowing her seeds today – one variety every couple of days. She liked to take her time with things she considered important; to savour the feeling she wasn't often privy to anymore. She didn't like having responsibility before she moved here; she couldn't handle the fact that the things she did might affect others in some inconceivable way that was completely out of her control. Her world had changed a while before everybody else's, and it had taken its toll.

Now here she was surrounded by nothing but the land, and while the harsh and unforgiving nature of it couldn't guarantee her safety, it could guarantee her anonymity; it would never rescue her, but it would never judge her, either. Here, she was free to assert herself, she was free to plant the seeds she'd harvested from last year's crops and do it in the way she thought best, sticking to her own schedule or, sometimes, no schedule at all. And if the crops didn't grow for whatever reason, there was no one else to feel the effect but her. There was no one to blame her. She could relinquish control to the land.

She took off her robe and pulled on her grey fleece. It smelled damp and stale – she'd been caught in a sudden downpour early last week that had soaked through her clothes before she made it back. She'd been collecting wood when the clouds had changed so rapidly that she hadn't even realised until she heard the soft drops against the forest floor, sporadic at first as they found their way through the canopy. Then she'd felt it, right on the tip of her nose as she looked up at the fractured pieces of darkening sky between the treetops.

She'd abandoned the wood in a pile to return to the following day and she'd ran as quickly as she could back down the hill to the edge of the river, through the cool waters that ran over rocks and stones, and back up the rutted bank on the other side. She ought to have pegged the fleece up to dry on the little wire that hung across the living room, but she'd been so cold, she could feel it in her bones. She'd shivered violently as she undressed and tried to light the fire, her fingers numb as she grappled with holding a match. Amidst all the chaos of the cruel nature of the wilderness, she'd tossed the fleece to one side and forgotten all about it until it was too late. Carelessness gets you killed in the wild, that's what Cal said. She sniffed at the sleeve – she would wash it in the river this afternoon then hang it out to dry in the sun.

There was still some water left over in the pan, cool now but clean; she carefully poured it into her chipped china mug and left it on the side to save for later. Her petrol supply was getting low, she couldn't afford to keep using the generator to boil water so she'd tried to limit herself to twice a day – half a pan in the morning and half a pan in the afternoon, unless it was wash day, then she would allow herself a full pan if she couldn't face the river.

It had been a particularly harsh January, relentlessly cold with bursts of heavy snow that had caught her by surprise – she'd used up a month's worth of her fuel supply in just two weeks. She couldn't go out and there was so little light, the clouds grey and heavy, full of the snow that kept on falling. She missed the days of the weather forecasts, she hadn't realised how much she'd relied on them until they were no longer there. She'd tried to read the skies and be at one with the land, to predict what was coming in a way she thought she'd learn, but then the snow came and she understood: she was at the mercy of Mother Nature, and she was unpredictable.

Ida pulled on her leggings, her socks and the old walking boots that had a hole in one side – the ones she saved for gardening or pottering around close to the house. She had another pair that Cal had found for her last year – she didn't ask where. They were brown with a pink trim and, more importantly, they were waterproof, so she saved them for when she had to wander further afield for wood or when she'd planned a long walk to clear her head and remind herself of the vastness of the world.

She stepped outside and used her binoculars to scan the front and the sides of the property, the way Cal had taught her. Then she walked round, past the wood store and the generator, and did the same at the back of the house, scanning the hills that ruled to the south. Ida didn't often walk in that direction, she didn't like the idea of coming to the peak and finding something on the other side, unexpectedly close and potentially deadly. The west felt safer, sheltered from what lay beyond by the thick forest and the dip in the land that led down to the river. The forest may hide things, but it also hid her, and she found a certain kind of solace in that. She explored the north and the east, too – miles of uninterrupted fields, leading to a distant horizon with nothing to speak of but more hills, but she never strayed too far.

She stood beside a large summer lilac, turning slowly from left to right, the heavy binoculars held with both hands. There was nothing to see – there never was – but that was no reason to lose focus; she needed to see properly, unhindered by her expectations. When she'd done one full sweep she turned slowly back to the left, checking one last time. Nothing. She took in the lilac next to her, yet to bloom. It was nicknamed the butterfly bush owing to its appeal to the insects; Ida spent many long, hot summer days just watching them arrive. The butterflies and the bees and everything in between. They were fascinating.

It had started off as a plant a few years ago, but it had quickly developed into a mass of shrubbery, thick branches reaching out, growing bigger each year. She'd cut it back last spring using the instructions in one of her gardening books and as she looked at it again now, she thought she might need to do the same. She didn't want her view from the bedroom at the back of her house to be obstructed by it, no matter how beautiful it looked in the summer. She felt one of the leaves between her thumb and forefinger, stroking the smooth surface. It reminded her of Cal; he'd turned up with a cutting in a bucket one summer afternoon, the first summer she'd been here. He said he'd found it during his travels and it had reminded him of her – bright and beautiful. Over the years, she'd also found it to be quite resilient and strong, but Cal had never commented on those attributes.

She took the binoculars back into the house and placed them on the little wooden table. In one of the kitchen cupboards she found the old tin where she kept her seeds, a picture of a West Highland terrier on the front and the words 'All Butter Shortbread' written in red. She tried not to look at the little picture of the crumbly biscuits but her mouth still watered at the memory of what they tasted like.

Inside, the seeds were neatly organised into little packets she'd saved from when they first arrived – tomatoes, lettuce and carrots. The packets were shop bought originally but the contents were now the result of hard work and dedication. She'd harvested every single one of them herself, year after year. She reached back into the cupboard and pulled out a canvas bag which she'd tied using the handles at the top. Inside were the potatoes she'd salvaged from last year's crop, twelve in total, all sprouting at odd angles. She took her time deciding which to plant first, considering her options.

Her gardening book advised planting the lettuce or the carrots first, but Ida had been aching for potatoes and was tempted to ignore the advice of the kind-looking man on the front of the book. She held one in her hand – the wrinkled potato the size of an egg. She imagined eating one of the new ones it would produce; a generous helping of melted butter on the top, a lush salad with coleslaw to the side and maybe some egg and cheese. Then she readjusted her cravings, making allowances for her circumstances – new potatoes, plain with a sprinkle of seasoning and perhaps a tin of mixed bean salad; she had two tins left in the kitchen cupboard below the sink. She'd never got this low before.

Aside from the mixed beans she had a large bag of pasta, two bags of rice, the odd tin of baked beans, soup and rice pudding, and a box of porridge oats. But the cupboards still looked sparse, much more so than they had ever looked before. If she was honest with herself, she was worried. He'd never been gone this long.

She held the little packets of seeds in her hands – lettuce in one, carrots in the other. She'd decided to take the book's advice and narrowed it down to the two recommendations. She would plant one today and one in a couple of days' time. She tried to recall the taste of freshly grown vegetables, the crispness of lettuce leaves or the sweetness of the carrots. She hadn't had anything fresh since blackberries last September. They'd grown in abundance in several of the bushes around the house and even more further afield. She'd added them to her porridge and used them to flavour her water; they'd stained her fingers and left their gritty seeds in her teeth. By the time they'd all shrivelled up she felt quite sure she would never long for another blackberry again. But she was wrong. As with most things in life, absence makes the heart grow fonder.

It had been almost four months since he'd visited – Christmastime – and even then he'd only stayed for a few days. He'd brought gifts wrapped in cloths – a couple of new books, a bottle of wine and a jigsaw. She wondered where he'd found them but didn't want to ask. There was a light dusting of snow on the ground and it crunched under their feet as they walked backwards and forwards to Cal's truck. He'd parked in the same place as usual, on a narrow dirt path over a mile away. You couldn't get any closer to the house than that, and it was still another three miles to the nearest road. The walk had felt longer, the crispness of the air stinging Ida's cheeks and the dampness of the grass clinging to her leggings.

Cal had brought her a large supply – much bigger than usual – and she knew then that he was preparing to be absent for some time, but they never spoke of it. Some things are better left unsaid, deprived of the life they would take on. They'd split the journeys over the three days he'd stayed, back and forth to the truck, loading backpacks and heaving huge cans of petrol. She'd thought Cal looked tired; the skin under his eyes was puffy and grey and he'd lost weight. She'd felt guilty for taking all of the food and had tried to feed him up while he was there, but he'd kindly refused all of her offers to serve him seconds and stuck to the same meagre portions she allowed herself.

She'd asked him several times about his life now, about the military and the survivors, the scientific developments and the political efforts, but he was reticent to go into much detail. It was Christmas, after all, he'd said. Ida felt deflated; he was her only source of information and she resented the lack of it. It unnerved her too, the absence of his usual reassurances. He'd told her there was no point in talking about the things he saw – the suffering, the death that permeated the streets, the chaos and devastation that it left. The dead weren't the unlucky ones, Ida knew enough to realise that. He wanted to protect her, he'd said, from the pain of it all. Ida noticed that his voice changed almost imperceptibly as he said this, a slight break in the strength of his words.

He'd told her he was doing all he could to help. He'd moved up the ranks and was now in charge of a team, ensuring law and order where the police had failed. He'd told her that people were like scavengers, trying to cling on to a life they no longer wanted, fighting in the streets over a meal. His eyes had shone in the light of the fire, damp and glassy with tears. 'Their desperation is what haunts me,' he'd whispered. Ida had shivered, her blood turning ice cold.

She'd lain her head on his chest, the feel of his thick wool jumper warm against her face. She'd fallen asleep listening to the sound of his heart beating, the steady rhythm gentle yet strong, reminding her of everything she missed.

CHAPTER THREE

S he worked slowly, turning over the soil then using her
forefinger to create long rows for the seeds. She'd chosen
lettuces in the end, spurred on by the fact that they grew
quickly and there was no preparation time with them – she
could just pluck them straight from the ground. She sprinkled
the seeds sparingly from the packet, using around a third. She
would plant some more in a few weeks, that way she could
prolong the harvest for as long as possible. Once the seeds were
scattered among the freshly turned earth, she used her hands to
sprinkle the soil and cover them up.

She needed to water them, but the rainwater tank was
empty. It had been an uncharacteristically dry March which
had eased seamlessly into the next month, with clear skies and
no sign of April showers on the horizon. The previous two years,
there had been ample water in the tank when it came to
planting. This year, there was only a thin layer left in the
bottom that clung to the corners and the bits of debris that had
worked their way in with the rain.

Ida grabbed her buckets and made her way down the bank
to the river. It had been hard work to begin with, the heavy

lifting and the constant physical effort of living this way – chopping fallen trees, carrying it to the wood store, planting and gardening and the maintenance of the house and the land. Ida had never done much of that kind of thing before, it had always been Cal. She'd been active, but not in the same way. Now, she saw muscles growing where she'd never had them before, in her arms and her thighs, now strong from the weight of the things she carried up and down the banks.

Ida watched her footing as she made her way down the uneven hill, looking out for potholes and sudden dips. Too many times she'd almost lost her balance and rolled her ankle. A muscle pull or a sprain would make her life considerably more difficult, she'd have to rest but the list of things she needed to do wouldn't wait. It was those kind of scenarios which sometimes kept her awake at night, particularly if she'd had a near miss that day. Before moving here, she would never have considered such things. If Cal was away for the night, it was murderers or burglars that worried her, not a sprained ankle or a broken arm.

Halfway down the hill Ida suddenly stopped, her senses on high alert. She'd heard something. It sounded like a high-pitched screech. Her mind's eye scanned her list of sounds, the birds and the wildlife, the wind and the water, but she couldn't match it to anything. She stayed as still as she could, hardly daring to breathe, the old buckets clutched tightly in her hands. She was at an angle, her feet pointing down towards the water, and she could feel it in her core, her torso beginning to strain under the weight of holding her back.

Then she heard it again. Ida's heart thrashed against her ribs, spurring her on, the adrenaline pumping, begging her to move. Still she stood there, not wanting to draw attention to herself. Very slowly, she looked from left to right, her eyes taking in the crest of the hill on the other side and the forest beyond, the endless fields to the right. From around a bend in the water, she saw a flash of white. It was a dog; big and shabby with patches of dirt on its face. She heard the sound again – it was a whistle, long and high-pitched.

Ida panicked. Dogs meant owners, which meant people. She let go of the buckets; one went rolling down the hill to the river while the other stayed behind her, caught on a tuft of holly bush. The dog stopped and stared at her, then it barked – a sound she hadn't heard in a long, long time; it made her jump. Ida turned on the hill and tried to run back to the house but in her haste to flee she tripped and landed heavily on her shoulder. The momentum of the fall propelled her downwards, towards the river, but before she made it all the way to the water she saw an obstacle in the way – a rock protruding awkwardly from the grass. It was too late, she couldn't stop herself rolling in time. She felt a sharp pain on the side of her head before the world began to blur, as though she were underwater.

And then there was nothing but darkness.

She dreamed of Cal. They were dancing. Bright lights lit up an otherwise dark room, multicoloured disco balls twisting and turning above them. The music was loud and fast but they were barely moving. They were floating around the dance floor as one, Ida's head resting against Cal's chest. She could smell his aftershave. She breathed it in, but the smell was intoxicating. It caught in her nostrils, heady and potent. What was it? Alcohol? She coughed, and as she tried to catch her breath the bright lights of the club fell away.

She sat up, her hand held to her mouth. She was in a room, dark and dingy with wooden walls and floors, towers of books lining the far side and a dead rabbit slung unceremoniously on a table under a window. The curtains were shut, if you could call them curtains – a piece of stained fabric nailed to the wall. Ida had been lying on a bed, a blanket pulled up to her waist. There was a sharp pain in the side of her head that made her feel sick. She tried to remember what had happened – the dog, the fall. Where was she?

She swung her feet out of the bed and onto the floor. She was still wearing her shoes and the clothes she'd had on before. She was gathering herself, edging closer to the side of the bed, trying to summon the strength to get to her feet and get out of wherever the hell she was. She was swaying, the dizziness forcing her to take her time when all she wanted to do was run as fast as she could, out of the door and as far away from here as possible.

The door opened with a sudden jolt, forcing her to jump up off the bed and onto unstable legs. Her knees buckled and she reached out for something to hold on to, but there was nothing there. It seemed to take her a long time to fall – she knew it was happening and she could see the old wooden floorboards coming closer to her, but she was powerless to stop it. She could see the world fading away – the man at the door hazy and unclear, the dog standing obediently at his side.

Ida had no idea how much time had passed but when she woke it was to bright sunlight filtering in through the window, the piece of material now hung back on one of the nails. She could see little flecks of dust dancing in the golden glare. The pain in her head had dulled, a throbbing ache rather than the nauseating sharpness from last time she'd come round.

She was lying on the bed, the checked blanket pulled up to her waist. She sat up slowly, taking in her surroundings. It was only when her eyes scanned to the far side of the room that she saw the man sat on a chair in the corner. He was watching her, a book in his hands and his sleeping dog lay at his feet.

Ida tried to think logically. The man looked feral – long unwashed hair blending in with his thick beard, a black T-shirt with a rip at the collar and bare feet that were caked with mud. He looked older than Ida, but not by much. Was he like her: living remotely to avoid civilisation? It certainly looked that way. It briefly occurred to Ida that she should be more concerned about his motive for bringing an injured and unfamiliar woman to his little hut than his potential for carrying the virus, but that's the way the world was now, the threat of disease more pronounced than the threat of more sinister intentions.

'You're awake,' the man said. His voice sounded gruff and dry, as though he wasn't used to using it.

'Where am I?' she asked.

'Your place is a couple of miles south from here.' He nodded vaguely in the direction of the door.

Ida didn't know whether he was telling her to go or not but she didn't want to wait around to find out. She got to her feet and didn't look back, pulling open the door and running out into the daylight. She looked around for any hint of familiarity but she couldn't see anything she recognised except for the river. She ran south for as long as she could, following the winding banks of the water's edge, before her body forced her to stop. Her mind kept telling her to run, to not stop until she was home, but she was exhausted. Her mouth was dry and her lungs stung with the sudden exertion.

She held her hand to her head, feeling where the pain was pulsating. There was something there, beneath her fingers. Something hard and matted in her hair. Was it glue? She looked back towards the hut, now hidden behind a patch of trees and undergrowth. Is that what the man had done – glued her head?

She carried on walking, relentless steps she barely had the energy to take. Eventually, she came to the familiar dirt track. She followed it west to the space where Cal usually parked his truck – she could see her house from here, a mile or so further south. She looked back towards the hut but it was completely hidden from view.

When she reached the perimeter she didn't open the gate. Instead, she headed straight down to the river, skirting the edges of the fence. She took off all of her clothes and washed them in the water, scrubbing at them then wringing them out and leaving them on the grass. Then she submerged herself in it, the cold water catching her breath as it ran through her hair and numbed the pounding at the side of her head. Then she got out and walked naked up to the house, pegging her clothes out on the little washing line and letting the afternoon sun dry her skin.

She was shivering, unable to control her body, but the compulsion to wash had far outweighed the discomfort of the cold. She needed to cleanse herself despite knowing that if the man was infected, she was already as good as dead. She pulled on her robe and climbed into bed, pulling the covers over her damp hair and wishing away the next few days; the painful agony of awaiting her fate.

CHAPTER FOUR

I t had been a difficult few days. Ida had convinced herself she was dying several times, infected in some cruel twist of fate by the only person besides Cal that she'd been anywhere near for more than three years. Her head pounded and felt heavy with the pain of it; every time she stood up she had to steady herself on the walls or the furniture. The cold from the river had seeped into her bones and stayed trapped there, her back and limbs aching with the memory of it. She was dizzy and dehydrated, and that only added to her concerns, her throat sore and dry and her vision blurred.

She slept as much as she could, restless nights turning into restless days. She used a bottle of her emergency water to tide her over and ate dry crackers and nuts from the cupboard. She dreamed of Cal often, and when she wasn't dreaming about him she was thinking about him, willing him to come to her. She missed him even more in her moments of weakness. On the fourth morning, Ida woke with a lighter head, the throbbing reduced to an uncomfortable but bearable bruising and the warmth restored to her bones. Even Ida had to admit she was probably out of danger by now. Her body was recovering from the fall but her mind would take time to catch up.

She ventured out to the vegetable garden, the soil pale and dry. She hoped she hadn't wasted the lettuce seeds – they needed water and nurturing. She glanced down towards the river, wondering if that's where the buckets still lay, but then she noticed them against the wall, one stacked inside the other. She frowned, trying to recall the day she fell. The buckets had definitely ended up down by the river – the only possible explanation, she realised, was that the man had moved them.

She'd been thinking about the stranger and what must have happened. He had to have carried her the few miles to his house, across the vast open space and up the slight incline in the land. She wondered why he hadn't just left her – he didn't know her; he didn't know whether she was ill or whether she'd had contact with the outside world. And even when he did decide to help her, why didn't he put her in her own bed? She looked north towards his hut, hidden from view entirely. He must have come back here and stacked the buckets for her. Had he been in her house too? It didn't look like anything had been moved or taken.

The man and his motives played on her mind while she walked down to the river with the buckets in her hands, her boots tied and her eyes on the ground beneath her. She walked slowly, checking and rechecking her footing, scared of the land for the first time in a while; she respected it, but she didn't fear it. She couldn't afford to, she needed it to survive.

Ida filled the buckets with the cold water that had cleaned her a few days earlier – the water that kept her alive. The man must use the same water source, she thought, further north where it was rougher and deeper. She lifted the buckets and began climbing back up the hill, taking regular breaks which she usually didn't need. The inactivity of the past few days had caused her back to seize; it ached along with her shoulders and her neck. She stopped and rolled her chin against her chest, feeling the pull reaching down into her spine.

She'd been careless, but she didn't realise it until she crested the peak of the hill. She hadn't used her binoculars the way she usually did, the way Cal had instilled in her that she must always do. Beside the perimeter, standing back from the gate she'd left open, stood the man and his dog.

'You're alive then,' he said, making no attempt to smile or come any closer. He leaned against one of the wooden posts, his mass of hair tied back off his face.

'What are you doing here?' Ida asked. She set the buckets of water down beside the fence and took a step back, away from the man, glancing over her shoulder as she did. She knew she could run south, towards the hills she didn't usually explore. Her go-bag was stuffed in an old compost bin at the back of the house, she could grab it and run.

'You ran off before I got a chance to tell you I superglued your head. Thought you might like to know.'

Ida instinctively touched the side of her head, wincing as her fingertips found the mass of hair now stuck there, matted and coarse.

'You bled a lot,' he told her. She didn't respond – she hadn't seen any blood, had he cleaned the wound? 'I sterilised it with alcohol,' he told her, as though reading her mind. Ida remembered the smell as she woke. 'You need to keep the area clean or it'll get infected.'

Ida still didn't respond, she just stood watching the man, wondering whether she should thank him or admonish him. It had been so long since she'd spoken to anyone other than Cal that she felt out of her depth.

The man nodded then turned to walk away, his dog following in his wake. Ida watched him, a hooded jacket tied around his waist, a long stick in his hand. Before she had a chance to think about it, she shouted after him, 'Do you live in that hut?'

He turned and looked at Ida, his eyes brimming with suspicion. He didn't answer for a while and Ida began to doubt whether he was going to at all. 'Yes,' he said simply. 'We won't be bothering you, don't worry.'

'We?' Ida asked. She hadn't seen anyone else while she was there.

'Yeah, me and Chief,' he answered, gesturing towards his dog.

'Oh. Okay.'

The quiet settled between them, neither of them needing to fill it – they were both well versed in comfortable silences. Then the man nodded once more and turned to leave. Ida watched him walk away, back towards the place she now knew existed, over the hill and a few miles north. She'd expected to feel uncomfortable, suffocated by the close proximity of another person nearby, but she was surprised to find that she didn't.

CHAPTER FIVE

Two weeks slipped by, her hair still matted but the cut underneath now healed. It still hurt her to lie on but the sharpness of the pain had waned. She'd got back to normality, tending to the vegetable patch daily. She'd planted some carrot seeds and a quarter of the potatoes and was watering them daily, making regular trips to the river. The consistency had eased the trepidation which had lingered in the days following the accident, the nervousness which sat heavily on her shoulders every time she'd walked slowly down the hill. Now, with the passing of time, it felt once again like part of her normal routine – just another task to complete.

It was another warm day, a gentle breeze whispering through the trees in the forest, crackling the new leaves that had appeared there. She loved it when it was like this, new life growing all around her, enough warmth to relax in but enough breeze to work in too. She tipped the water from the buckets into the rainwater tank then used the little tap to half fill the watering can.

She was carrying it around the side of the house when she heard something – a noise she couldn't quite identify. It made her spin around in the direction it had come from and in doing so she dropped the watering can, knocking it over. A couple of birds that had been pecking at the grass nearby took flight, spooked by the noise.

Ida looked around, her eyes wide and wild, her body pumped with adrenaline. Something moved in the distance, a dark spot in the middle of the fields to the north – towards the track. She told herself not to get her hopes up – it wasn't guaranteed to be Cal. She set the watering can down by the door and ran inside to grab her binoculars.

She stood on the step and pointed them at the distant shape which was moving steadily closer, working its way through the tall grass. It was him – she was sure of it. But she couldn't run to him, not yet, not until she was absolutely certain. The thought crossed her mind that it could be the stranger from the hut, but she could see enough to know that it wasn't – there was no mane of dark hair and no golden-white dog at his heels.

Another minute passed but the shape was still indistinguishable. A man, but faceless. She was itching to run to him; she could barely contain her excitement. It had been such a long time and only now that he was so close did she realise how far away he'd begun to seem to her. She'd forgotten his smell and the way he laughed. Her memories were fading, but the way she felt about him had only deepened.

Another couple of minutes passed and she heard the noise again.

'Ida!'

It was him, it was really him. She set the binoculars down on the step and took off, running across the fields with wild abandon, desperate to touch him, to feel his warmth and see his smile. As she drew closer, he put down the fuel cans he'd held in his hands. She didn't slow down, she just carried on running, not caring about how hard she hit him or how heavy they fell.

'There you are!' he shouted.

Her legs left the ground and wrapped around his body, holding him tighter than she thought herself capable. She nestled her face into the curve of his neck and inhaled, feeling the prickle of his hair as she kissed his skin. She felt weightless, her tiny frame eclipsed by Cal's.

'Pleased to see me?' He was holding her with ease, his strong arms a barrier between them and the world.

'You've been gone for so long,' she said, her eyes damp with tears. 'Too long.'

He eased his hold on her, lowering her to the ground. Her lace had come undone – she was amazed she hadn't tripped as she'd ran awkwardly over the uneven ground, abandoning all sense of herself, her arms flailing at her sides. She bent down to tie them, her fingers covered in soil, her nails black underneath. She wished she'd had some forewarning about his arrival; she would have washed and brushed her hair, put on something that didn't smell damp and stale and tidied up the house. But he had no way of letting her know, she was completely shut off from the world.

'I missed you.' He pulled her into him, tucking her hair behind her ear and kissing her hard. His beard tickled her face, the coarse hairs scratching at her skin in ways she had begun to forget.

'I missed you too.' She pulled away as his hands began to drift into her hair. The clump of glue remained knotted near her scalp, invisible to the eye but not to the touch. It wasn't really until that exact moment that Ida realised she'd made a decision – she wasn't going to tell Cal about the accident. She didn't want to worry him. 'Let's go up to the house, I'll make you a drink.'

He bent to pick up the fuel tanks, one in each hand, waving

away Ida's attempts to help him. 'You'll never guess what I've found for you.'

'What?' Ida asked, excited at the prospect of a surprise. The last time he'd said that he'd brought her some chocolate and a bottle of Southern Comfort, the latter of which she still had half a bottle of tucked away in her kitchen cupboard.

'Wait and see,' he told her.

They ambled back towards the house, the four hundred metres or so of overgrown fields, the grass wild and patchy and the soil beneath hard and dry.

'How have you been?' she asked him. She couldn't wait for the formality of sitting down to chat, she needed to know. She could tell Cal wanted to wait; he wanted to enjoy the moment before he told her about the reality he tried so desperately to shield her from. He'd told her before that it would overwhelm her if he shared everything straight away; three years of peace and quiet then the worries of the world just dumped on her. He had a point. Ida often felt her heart rate quicken and her breathing turn shallow when he told her about the horrors he'd experienced since his last visit, but that seemed like a small price to pay, and a very necessary one. She *should* know what her partner was going through; she should be able to share that burden.

'I'm okay,' Cal told her, lowering the fuel tanks and readjusting his grip. 'How have you been? Any trouble?'

'I'm okay. I'm low on supplies though, down to my last tank of fuel.'

'Good timing then,' he said sheepishly. 'Sorry it's been a while, I wanted to get here sooner.'

'It's okay,' she said, not knowing whether she meant it.

'Have you seen anyone?'

'No one until recently.' He looked sideways at her, his eyes full of concern, but he didn't say anything, just waited for her to continue. 'A couple passed through about a month ago, coming from the south then heading through the forest. They didn't come close, it looked like they were carrying a tent and supplies.'

'Probably sleeping rough,' Cal said.

'That's what I thought. Then I saw a man a few weeks ago with a dog, he came from the north.'

Cal looked over his shoulder in the direction she'd just indicated. 'Did he come up to the perimeter?'

'No,' she replied. 'He didn't come that close.' Her stomach turned uneasily. She wasn't used to lying to Cal, she never had any reason to. Yet here she was, lying about the biggest thing to happen to her in the entirety of her being here.

Cal had put a perimeter around the house in the early days – it had taken him a month of tireless work, every day in all weathers. It ran around the property at a safe distance. They'd painted signs and Cal had nailed them to the posts at regular intervals, warning any passers-by to stay away. Every time Ida went beyond the perimeter she had to use one of the three gates – one to the north, east and west.

'Have you seen him again since?' Ida waited too long to answer, beginning to doubt herself and her decision to lie to him. She saw Cal tense as he noticed her hesitation; small and fleeting but so obvious to him. 'Ida?' he prompted.

'I think so, a few days later. But I haven't seen him since.'

Cal was quiet for a moment, thinking about what she'd told him. Ida knew it wouldn't be the last conversation they had about strangers passing through, but for now he seemed to let it go. 'All the signs still up?' he asked.

'Yes, but they're fading.'

'I noticed. I'll bring paint next time.'

'How long are you staying?' Ida tried to keep the emotion out of her voice, she didn't want to allay her own anxieties by putting them onto him. She knew he was needed back out there.

He took a deep breath before he answered and she took it as a sign that she wasn't going to like what he had to say. 'I can't stay long, Ida. A couple of days? Maybe three. I can't be gone longer than a week.'

She knew he would have already isolated himself somewhere remote for a few days before he visited; he would have wanted to make sure he wasn't carrying any of the virus before he got close to her. She also knew it was a whole day's travelling to get to her, and to get back to wherever it was he was going next.

'Where have you been?'

'London, mostly, and the surrounding areas. There's a big military zone there now, bigger than last time I was here. There's one in Manchester and Birmingham too, and there's talk of setting one up in Leeds, if it's needed.'

'That sounds promising.'

'We'll see,' Cal said. Ida knew he didn't want to get her hopes up; there'd been promising signs before that had ended up fading away to nothing.

They reached the house and he put the tanks down next to the wood store. 'You're low on wood,' he said.

'I know, I had to use most of my supply in January.'

'Bad weather?' he asked.

'Terrible. The worst snow I've ever seen.'

He slipped his backpack off of his shoulders and put his hands on his hips, surveying the area slowly. 'I'll help you get stocked up while I'm here. Rainwater tank working okay?'

Ida nodded. 'I'll get you a drink.' She went inside and grabbed the mug of water she'd set aside that morning, drinking a small amount herself before taking it out to Cal. 'Here.'

'Thanks,' he said, taking it and gulping it down in one go. 'That reminds me,' he said, passing the mug back to Ida. He bent down to his rucksack and began rummaging through the contents. Then, from the middle of his bag, protected by one of his jumpers, he took out a glass jar, half full with brown granules. He stood and passed it to her, beaming.

'Coffee?' she said, staring at the label. *Kenco Smooth.* 'Oh my God, where did you get this?'

'One of the guys found it so I traded him.'

Ida didn't ask what he'd had to sacrifice, she just stepped towards him, the coffee in one hand and the mug in the other, and kissed him hard on the lips. 'Thank you. I need to go and get some water, then I'll make us one!' She felt giddy at the thought of it.

'I'll come with you,' he said. 'But afterwards we need to go to the truck and pick up some more supplies.'

She breathed deeply, trying not to let his words land – the words that reminded her that they're not just a normal couple enjoying a retreat in the wilderness, about to have a nice hot coffee in the afternoon sun. They're a couple who need supplies, a couple who are on limited time. For just a moment – an hour, maybe two – she needed to allow herself the simple pleasure of denial.

CHAPTER SIX

I t didn't have the milk and the sugar she'd usually take it with, and she used only half of a teaspoon of coffee, but the smell alone would have been comforting enough. It reminded her of working, sat marking papers in the staffroom with the low hum of children playing outside. She breathed in the steam, enjoying its bitterness. She looked over the table at Cal. He was watching her with his blue-grey eyes, narrowed the way they always were when he was taking something in.

'What?' she asked.

'Just making sure I remember this moment.'

She lifted the mug to her lips and sipped. Like with most things in life now, she didn't want to rush it. Cal had already drained his mug – the china one with a picture of a camper van on the side, the one that stayed in the cupboard for long stretches of time until he arrived – and Ida suspected it wasn't the first taste he'd had; she felt sure he wouldn't have been able to resist a cup while he was hunkered down alone somewhere out in the wilderness. She didn't begrudge him that, it only made him more human to her. It was easy to think of him as surprisingly less so nowadays – he was like a machine, going through the motions of his new-found heroism, saving the world and everyone left in it. But here he was, just a man, and she loved him all the more for it.

'We'd better get going,' Cal said, walking over to the kitchen counter and placing his empty mug down. Ida felt a wave of resentment – why couldn't he let her enjoy this moment? She didn't ask for much – but she immediately felt selfish for thinking it, knowing how much it took for him to come here – the organising, the stress of travelling, the time away from his work and what that cost him. She could see it in his eyes – the distraction. Something was going on, something that he'd had to leave behind to come to her.

Ida finished her coffee and left the mug beside Cal's on the side. It was simple things like this she missed – two mugs instead of one, sharing her space and everything in it with someone she loved. 'Okay, I'm ready.'

They walked north, beyond the perimeter, towards the track. They didn't see anyone, just a couple of rabbits grazing on the fields and the odd bird rummaging through the grass for food. Ida found herself scanning the surrounding fields, looking for the man and his dog but hoping she wouldn't see them. She wondered what would happen if she did. Would the man approach her and ask her how her wound was healing? Then she would have to explain everything to Cal and hope that he wouldn't carry the weight of it back to the outside world. She shuddered at the thought of her accident causing him to lose concentration, to overlook something that would jeopardise his safety. Out there, she needed him sharp and focused; at his best. She couldn't risk losing him.

It didn't take long to reach the familiar Jeep that Cal had owned for as long as she knew him. It was old and battered, covered in a thin layer of dust and countless scratches and dints. The number plate was one he'd had since his twenty-first birthday, many years before he met Ida. It was personalised with his name followed by a few numbers and had cost him more than a month's wage. The interior of the truck was crammed full of supplies; Ida's stomach turned, a heavy weight resting on her shoulders at the realisation of what this meant.

'There's a lot.'

'Yeah.' Cal scratched his head, opening the passenger side door. 'Thought I'd stock you up... just in case.'

They both knew what just in case meant. It meant that he wouldn't be back for a long time. Another four months, maybe more. She tried to remember how much there'd been the last time he came; a similar amount, maybe, but that had been for the winter – more fuel and candles, firelighters and some new clothes for Ida.

'Here.' Cal handed her an old shopping bag – one of the big reusable ones with a picture of groceries on the side. It had seen better days. She looked inside – it was full of pasta and rice in clear plastic bags. She frowned. 'What's wrong?' he asked.

'If I never saw pasta or rice again I wouldn't complain.' Then, worried she sounded ungrateful, she added: 'I mean, thank you, this is great, it's just...'

Cal interjected. 'No need to explain, I feel exactly the same. Unfortunately, I'm afraid your theory will be tested soon enough.' She looked at him questioningly. 'We don't have an unlimited supply. That stuff's probably past its best as it is.'

'It's running out?'

'It's running out.'

She felt silly now, and naïve and selfish and all of the things she so often felt. 'But... what will we do?'

'We're really pushing to grow crops this year and find some solution to the food shortages. Have you started planting?' He hauled a rucksack onto his back and heaved a couple of fuel tanks out of the car. Ida grabbed one.

'Yes, a couple of weeks ago.'

'Spread them out as much as you can.'

'I will. Has there been any progress at all? Any hope?' She was desperate for some good news.

Cal pulled another bag out from the back seat then shut the doors and locked the truck. 'Not really.'

'Tell me,' she pleaded.

They began walking back towards the house.

'There's not much to tell. It's grim, Ida. It's a living hell. For every person we help, there's another we're unable to. Everyone has lost someone; there are orphans all over the country and very few adults able to care for them.'

'But you said they're expanding the military zones?'

'That's the plan,' he said, pausing for a moment before adding: 'But they're just a temporary measure really.'

Ida felt sick and she knew she'd heard enough. Cal saw it too, in the quickening of her pace and the way her eyes dropped down to the ground, unable to look at the world and believe it could be so cruel.

'Tell me about you,' Cal said, wanting to change the conversation. 'How's life been here?'

Considering what she'd just heard, she couldn't complain. So she didn't, even though she wanted to. 'Things are okay. It was a long winter but I managed. Slept in front of the fire a lot but I had to use the backup heater when the wood supply started running out.'

'It uses a lot of fuel.' There was no hint of criticism in his voice – she knew he would never suggest she was being wasteful; he knew her better than that – he was just stating a fact, one she already knew too well. 'You look good,' he said. 'Strong.'

She'd thought the same about him. He looked muscly, his broad shoulders even broader than she'd remembered. She'd been worried about him the last time he'd visited, he'd lost weight and looked tired. She was pleased to see he was looking healthier this time. 'You too,' she said.

'There's been a lot to do. It keeps me fit, I suppose.'

She wondered what he'd been doing but didn't want to ask; every time she tried to talk to him about the outside world it either seemed to push him away or make her withdraw. So instead she told him about the last four months – about the river that froze over and the crow that had visited her all winter. She told him about the helicopter that had flown low across the fields and landed somewhere in the distance. She'd added the sound of it to her list.

'Probably military,' Cal said.

'I thought so.'

She didn't tell him about the accident or how the man had helped her, even though she knew it was a big secret to keep from him. There was something holding her back – something more than what she'd initially thought. It wasn't just about protecting him from the inevitable worry; she felt *silly*, for having the accident to begin with and then for needing to be saved. She didn't want Cal to think of her as weak or vulnerable, she liked the Ida he saw when he looked at her now: capable; strong; bright. She didn't want to taint that with the truth.

They completed two supply runs before they called it a day, hot and sweaty from the effort and their stomachs grumbling with hunger.

'Tonight, madam, I shall be cooking you the house special – pasta with sauce!' Cal took a jar of pasta sauce out of one of the bags and held it out to her. 'Tomato and herb.'

She laughed, and as she heard herself she was shocked by how unnatural it sounded. How long had it been since she last laughed? She sat at the kitchen table and watched him work, boiling the water they'd collected from the river and adding the pasta, then straining it before adding the sauce.

They ate in a comfortable silence, enjoying each other's company and the food. Ida had skipped lunch – something she'd been doing increasingly often lately – and her stomach had the empty, hollow feeling she'd grown so accustomed to. It would be nice to go to bed with a full belly for a change, lethargic under the weight of a proper meal.

Cal insisted on washing the pots outside using what was left in the rainwater tank. Ida undressed and washed using some cool boiled water, hunched over the kitchen sink with a bar of soap. Then she cleaned her teeth, put on her robe and lit some candles in the bedroom. When Cal came in to her, he didn't speak. They just lay down and looked at each other, their noses almost touching. He'd aged, she thought, the lines around his eyes becoming deeper and his dirty blond hair streaked with more grey. She brushed her hands through it, then traced her fingertips around the outline of his jaw, through his coarse beard and down to his chest.

She wanted him, and he wanted her, but they often did this dance to begin with: Cal too guilty for the time he'd spent away to make a move, and Ida carrying too much pride to take control. It was like the early days of their relationship, every time they came back together this way – the little touches that caught her breath, the long kisses that led to nowhere and the limbs entwined so tightly she could no longer tell where she ended and he began. Ida loved it and she hated it. She loved feeling him close to her but hated knowing she would feel his absence all the more once he left – in the empty space beside her, in the singular mug on the kitchen counter and in the silence that ran through the house. She loved feeling his arms wrapped around her, but she hated knowing that it was only for a small moment in time. Was it worth it? She asked herself the same question almost daily; she'd even asked Cal once.

It was summertime, a little over a year since he'd first left. He'd been gone for eight weeks and it was the longest stretch she'd been alone. She'd ached for him. She'd felt so lonely and isolated that she began to question whether there was anyone left – surely she would *feel* it, the presence of others somewhere in the world. But she didn't. She felt so acutely alone that it became physically painful. She pleaded with forces beyond her control to return him safely to her. She was desperate to hear his voice and to tell him the things that had sat so heavily in her mind. It was the first thing she'd said to him when he'd arrived, through tears which wouldn't wait for him to hold her.

'Is it worth it?' He'd looked surprised, his brow creasing. 'All the pain of missing you. Is it worth it, just for these small moments in time?'

'Is that the way you feel?'

'Yes. Don't you?'

'No. The time away from you is to keep you safe. And the time I spend with you is my reward.'

'But I don't feel that way. I *can't* feel that way because you won't let me help. I'm just sat here waiting for you.'

'I need to know you're safe so I can focus, Ida, we've been over this. Out there, among the chaos and the devastation, I would only be able to think of you and the danger you'd be in. I wouldn't be able to do my job. So if you're there, I might as well not be.' She hadn't responded so he'd carried on talking, filling the silence that hung between them. 'Coming here, knowing that you're waiting for me somewhere safe... it's everything. You *are* helping. You're helping more than you know. So yes, it's worth it. You're worth it.'

She hadn't asked him again but she'd wondered the same

question many times since, always to herself. She wondered whether she would be better off telling him not to visit her anymore, to leave the supplies by the gate and let her get on with living. The trouble was, without Cal, could she call it living? Would she just be existing? She wouldn't have the constant voice in her head which tried to convince her he wouldn't be coming back this time; that he was dead or had forgotten about her. But she wouldn't have something to look forward to either. She wouldn't have someone to hold, no matter how intermittently.

It was a balance, she reasoned. Sometimes she thought she would be better off with the consistency of her loneliness, without the contrast of Cal's company to remind her what she was missing. But other times, she thought, she was just happy to have him lie next to her, sharing her bed and her house and the world that they'd created.

CHAPTER SEVEN

She woke to an empty space beside her, her bare arm stretched out across the bed in the place where Cal should be. She threw back the covers and padded barefoot across the wooden floor, her heart hammering in her chest. She stepped into the kitchen hoping to find him making breakfast, but all she saw was the watery light filtering in through the window, casting long beams across the floor. It was empty.

'Cal?' she shouted. 'Cal!'

She spun around in a full circle for reasons which defied logic, as though she was hoping he would somehow materialise from nowhere. When that didn't work she opened the door and tentatively stepped outside, onto the grass which was still damp with morning dew. She looked around, west to east and then back again, but all she saw was the empty space which usually greeted her, the empty space full of nothing which mattered when Cal was here.

'Cal?' she tried again. As she stood there shouting his name she suddenly realised that they hadn't finished transporting the supplies; Cal would never leave before that was done. She put her hand to her forehead, shielding her eyes from the low sun.

She looked north towards the track, hoping to see him ambling back towards her, arms full of the things he'd brought for her. But he wasn't there.

She put on her walking boots – the ones without the hole in – and started heading in the direction of the truck. She pulled her robe closed tighter around her and double knotted the tie. Some days she didn't bother to get dressed, she couldn't see the point, especially over the colder months when she idled away her time reading or doing sudoku, or starting one of the jigsaws that Cal had brought her.

She passed through the perimeter, opening and closing the gate, and carried on walking north. It was a steady incline to the track, one you could hardly notice until you looked back to where you'd started, the one-storey house lost among the landscape. Halfway up she could just make out the truck, but there was no sign of Cal. She carried on walking, her pace quickening as panic gripped her. Had something happened?

When she reached the truck the first thing she did was try the doors – locked. She rested her forehead against the cool glass of the window, watching as her breath steamed in front of her. All the supplies were still there. She walked round to the other side of the truck and fixed her eyes into the distance, scanning from left to right.

There were people there – two of them. She squinted, trying to get a better view, but the glare of the sun was distorting them, covering them in a hazy glow. She used her hand to block it.

It was Cal – she recognised his blue windbreaker. The other man was taller but slimmer, a dog at his heels. Ida recognised him as the man from the hut, the stranger who'd superglued her head. Her stomach sank – what could they possibly be talking about? The man was wearing a khaki hoody and was carrying a long stick in his hand, his hair loose and unkempt, blowing in the wind. Cal was standing close to him – too close, she thought. He didn't have his suit on to protect him; why was he taking the risk? She hadn't had any choice in the matter when she'd woke up in his bed, slipping in and out of consciousness, but Cal didn't need to be this close to him... or did they know each other?

'Cal!' she shouted, waving her arms in the air.

She saw him turn to face her, momentarily turning back to the man before jogging towards her and the truck. The man, she noticed, watched as Cal moved further and further away from him, briefly looking at her as she stood just in front of the truck. When Cal had almost reached her, the man turned and walked away, towards the road which lay miles to the north. Towards his hut. She had so many questions; she had to take a long, steadying breath before she trusted herself to sound coherent. She was worried, she realised, in case Cal had found out about the accident. She'd chosen to keep it from him for good reason and she didn't like the idea of him finding out this way, from a stranger rather than from her.

'Who is that?' she asked first, quickly followed by: 'Do you know him?'

Cal smiled, but he didn't answer straight away, he just looked at her. She was suddenly aware of what she must look like in her walking boots and robe combination, her hair wild and untamed from sleep.

'I forgot how beautiful you look in the morning,' he said.

'Cal! Who is that?' She gestured with her hand towards the man and his dog, hoping that he wouldn't be able to answer her.

'He was asking questions.' Ida knew he was debating how much to tell her, his instinctual need to protect her weighing heavily on him – she was aware that he was constantly trying to strike the right balance, to arm her with a certain amount of truth but not so much that it would overwhelm her.

'About?'

'Just the land and supplies. Wanting information, like everyone else.'

Ida's forehead creased, surprised by this answer. The man hadn't seemed interested in anything of Ida's, in fact, he'd seemed particularly disinterested. He'd returned to the house to collect her buckets and stack them by the wall but he hadn't taken anything from her – at least not that she could tell. Had he rummaged around, trying to find out just how much she had? Had Cal's presence piqued his interest? Maybe he'd seen the truck full of goods and decided he'd like some of them for himself.

'Is he dangerous?'

Cal scratched his head and looked over his shoulder, towards the man and his dog who were continuing north. Ida could see the thick treeline which looked like a border from this distance, as though it were lining a field or marking out a boundary. She'd never paid much attention to it before but now she knew what was hiding behind it she wondered how she'd missed it – or how Cal had.

'I don't think he'll come back, but if he does, you need to get as far away from him as possible – we don't know enough about him to trust him.'

'But... but you were standing right next to him...'

'He's a recluse, he hasn't been near civilisation for God knows how long.'

She'd guessed as much herself by the way that he lived – his tiny hut only sparsely filled – and by his appearance – rough and rugged. A loner. A hunter.

'Okay,' Ida said, relieved that her secret was safe.

Cal stepped towards her and brushed her hair off her face, tracing his fingers down her cheek and to her lips. 'Everything's okay,' he said. Ida knew that it was a lie – but one with good intentions.

'Okay,' whispered Ida.

He bent down and kissed her, moving his hand to the back of her head, his fingers entwined in her red hair. She thought about the matted section at the side, ready to move away if his fingers ventured too close, but they didn't. Ida moved closer to him, her chest against his body, feeling his warmth. Stood on the crest of a hill in the arms of the man she loved, Ida felt all her worries escaping, released into the surroundings she thought of as her own. She knew they would wait for her, her worries, ready to consume her once more when Cal had left, but for now she felt lighter than she had done in a long time.

Cal cooked again, keeping to no schedule but their own internal one, their stomachs rumbling as the sun rose high and bright in the sky. She enjoyed watching him potter around the tiny kitchen space, setting bowls on the counter and heating up the contents of the pan. Before this house, they'd rented a two-bed terrace in Surrey, a twenty-minute drive from Ida's mum and an hour away from London. They'd been living there for almost a year when they'd had to leave; Ida had sat quietly as Cal reversed his truck off the drive, the back crammed full of their things. Tears had ran down her cheeks as she watched the familiar streets turn to unfamiliar roads. She'd wanted to scream wildly just to fill the silence that sat heavily between them, but she couldn't. She could barely move, the weight of her worries paralysing her. Cal didn't speak either, lost in his own fears and his need to protect Ida, to get as far away from the cities and people as possible. There'd been an announcement almost a month before, the

Prime Minister ordering people to stay at home, but what had followed had done little to appease their anxieties. Hospitals were overrun, supermarket shelves were almost empty. Societal unrest was increasing. It was Cal who'd suggested that they leave. He'd found somewhere remote; somewhere they could hunker down and wait for the storm to pass.

Ida still thought about their house now – the cast-iron fireplace; the window seat in the bedroom where she liked to sit and read; the roll-top bath she'd relax in most evenings. But more than anything, she remembered Cal cooking a Sunday roast in the kitchen while she pottered about the house, pegging out the washing or looking over his shoulder to see how long it would be. The radio would be on loud and she would dance around to the latest music, a glass of wine in her hand.

Depending on what kind of mood she was in, the memories of the time before could either make her smile or they could make her cry. Most of the time she didn't allow herself to dwell on things she no longer had, they didn't serve her well out here. But right now, with Cal nearby, she only smiled.

They ate outside, sat cross-legged on the rough grass at the front of the house, a bowl of rice resting on makeshift trays and a light breeze lifting the ends of Ida's hair. She noticed Cal's eyes glance into the distance on more than one occasion, towards the truck and the man with the dog. Towards the hut she wasn't sure he knew was there.

'We need to go back,' he said once they'd finished. 'We need to get the rest of the supplies.' He took a long drink of water then got up and held out his hand for Ida's bowl. She knew he was worried that the man would return before they did – there was still enough in the truck to entice anyone who'd been living in such harsh, solitary conditions for so long. But her understanding didn't ease her trepidation; she wanted to keep Cal as far away from the man as possible for reasons she couldn't confide in him; reasons which she had to keep hidden.

'Okay.' She handed him her bowl and stood up beside him, resigned to the fact that there was no alternative.

On their way back to the truck, Ida now dressed in her leggings and a light jumper, Cal suddenly stopped and turned to her, taking her face in his hands and kissing her deeply.

'I do miss you, you know that don't you?' His eyes narrowed as he looked at her, searching for something Ida wasn't sure she had anymore.

'I miss you too,' she said.

'I know it might not seem like it when you're out here all alone, but I think about you every day.' He pulled a chain from out of his T-shirt; it hung loosely around his neck, long and silver with a small circular locket attached to the end. He opened it, revealing a compass in one side and a photo of Ida in the other. The picture was from their first camping trip together; she was sat on top of a hill smiling at him, her hair braided and her eyes full of excitement. She almost didn't recognise herself. 'I kiss you every morning and every night.'

Ida smiled. 'You do?' He'd never told her that before; she knew about the locket, she knew he looked at it often, but knowing he kissed her morning and night made her cheeks flush. It was easy to forget he could be suffering in the same ways she was, missing her and grieving for the time they would never get back. She'd come to think of him as too busy and important to remember her while he was away, though if she really thought about it, deep down, she knew that wasn't true. Perhaps it was a protective mechanism – she couldn't afford to take on his pain as well as her own. Yet here she was, smiling that their grief was shared.

'Of course I do.'

Ida reached out her hand and held it against his cheek,

stroking the hairs which grew there with her thumb. 'I want this all to be over,' she said.

'I know. Me too.' He took her hand in his and brought it to his mouth, kissing it. 'We have to keep believing things will get better. We have to have hope, okay? Promise me?'

'I promise,' she whispered, unsure whether she could actually commit to something so significant. Did she have any hope left anymore? She thought that maybe, somewhere, there was a small amount. Somewhere dark and hidden but ultimately safe.

'I love you,' he said, pulling her into him and holding her close.

She wrapped her arms around him, and as she did so she felt her broken heart mending just a little bit. She couldn't help thinking how incredibly cruel it was that any progress would soon be undone, her heart shattering once more, a thousand fragile pieces scattering among the emptiness that he would leave behind.

CHAPTER EIGHT

E ach morning she woke in limbo: would today be their last day together? On the third day, the limbo became more of a painful certainty. They'd lain in bed together in a comfortable silence, enjoying the temporary reprieve from their loneliness, refusing to acknowledge what would follow.

'Breakfast in bed for my love.' Cal walked into the bedroom carrying two plates and wearing nothing but his underwear despite the cool start to the morning. The sunlight flooded in through the little window as Ida pulled back the curtains beside her bed, highlighting his toned chest and the coarse blond hairs which grew there.

'I could get used to this,' she said, then, seeing Cal's expression drop, she immediately regretted it. 'Thank you, it looks delicious.' She forced more cheeriness into her voice than she really felt, wanting their last morning together to be one he could remember fondly.

He'd brought her some eggs from the chickens they had at the military camp; he'd scrambled them and served them with some tinned plum tomatoes and a sprinkle of pepper. Ida's mouth watered, she hadn't had eggs in a long time. They'd tried keeping chickens to begin with but twice the foxes had got to them – the second time it hadn't even taken them all; she'd woke to two dead carcasses by the wood store, a trail of blood encircling them. She'd sat and cried when she found them, then she'd buried them at the back of the house.

She'd made the mistake of growing quite fond of the chickens. They were friendlier than she'd imagined – often they would follow her around the gardens and hop onto her lap when she sat down – she'd grown to think of them as her pets rather than a source of food, and the responsibility and accountability she'd felt for them had haunted her as she dug their graves. Blameless or not, she'd felt the searing guilt as though she'd killed them herself.

When Cal offered to bring her some more, Ida quickly refused. She knew death was occurring on a huge scale in the rest of the world but she didn't need it to happen right outside her house. Perhaps they'd try again at some point, when Cal had the time to build something sturdier to keep them in, but for now she was happy to just enjoy what was in front of her – scrambled eggs without the responsibility and eventual blame. She noticed Cal hadn't put any on his own plate – it looked bare, just a few tomatoes and a couple of crackers.

'Why haven't you got any eggs?' she asked.

'They're for you, baby,' he said simply, shrugging.

She smiled and scooped up another spoonful. 'They're so good.' She realised she was talking with her mouth full of food but she didn't care, in that moment she wanted to both talk and eat and she knew there wasn't much time left, certainly not enough to care about manners or etiquette. At the back of her mind she recognised the familiar thoughts, the ones that always came when time was running out, telling her to keep him busy, to love him harder than ever and distract him from reality – maybe then he would lose track of time.

'I need to leave today, Ida. I don't want to, but I can't stay any longer.'

Ida felt as though he'd read her mind and she scolded herself for thinking about him leaving; she'd never been very good at hiding her feelings, she wore them on her face and in her eyes even when she didn't speak them. 'I know,' she said. She stared down at her empty plate, determined not to let him see her cry. She wanted his memories of her to be happy ones that would help him through the months ahead and lift him up when he was feeling down; she didn't want him to have to worry about her. She didn't want to be a burden.

'I'm going to walk to the forest and help you stock up on wood...'

Ida interrupted. 'It's spring, Cal. I don't need the wood until autumn.'

'It needs to dry in the wood store. It's always better to be proactive rather than reactive.' Cal got up from the bed and pulled on his T-shirt and shorts. 'What if there's an uncharacteristically bad summer? What if you need it early on in the autumn and it's still wet? What if the generator packs up?'

Ida sighed, knowing that this wasn't an argument she could win. She didn't want to spend their last hours together going back and forth to the forest, picking through the wood, chopping fallen trees and stacking it all up by the house. She wanted to keep him beside her in bed, their bodies entwined as they had been all night.

Cal took Ida's empty plate from her and carried the pots back into the kitchen. 'I'm going to make us a coffee,' he shouted through to the bedroom. 'Then we'll get to work.'

They'd done this routine many times before: Cal wanting to fill their remaining hours with movement and purpose while Ida wanted to fill them with stillness and silence, just appreciating his presence in her space, knowing she could reach out and touch him or ask him a question if she wanted to. She liked to hear the gentle rhythm of his breathing; sometimes at night, she would lie awake just listening to the rise and fall of his chest, watching the occasional flicker of his eyes. Sometimes she would rest her head on him and listen to his heart while putting a hand on her own, wondering whether they were in sync. This was the hardest part, Ida thought, waiting for him to go. It felt somehow crueller than waiting for him to arrive, but she knew she would probably change her mind about that after he'd gone.

On one of his visits, Cal had left in the early hours before Ida had woke. A couple of days before, she'd told him how difficult she found their goodbyes, so he'd decided to take it upon himself to make it easier for her. He'd written her a note, scribbled in the margins of one of her sudoku puzzles, and left it in the empty space he'd left behind, tucked under Ida's arm.

This is not a goodbye note, it's a good morning one.
Cal x

Two months later, during a summer shower, he'd emerged from the north carrying the usual supplies, a questioning look on his face as though he'd been wondering for all the time he'd been gone whether he'd done the right thing. Ida had told him never to do it again; as hard as she found the goodbyes, she also needed them. They anchored her – the end to their hellos. Cal had made her a promise, drenched by the rain and with his hand on his heart. 'I promise I will always say goodbye.'

They spent several hours walking back and forth to the

forest, up and down the dip and across the river. Each time they walked down the slope together she remembered her accident and thought of the man from the hut and the secret she was keeping from Cal. She wondered if she would ever tell him how he'd helped her – perhaps once this was all over and they were back in their little house in Surrey, tucked up in bed on a lazy Sunday morning. Maybe then she'd tell him, confident that it wouldn't affect him in their comfortable life on the other side. He'd laugh about it, probably, and tell her he always knew she was clumsy. Or he'd be horrified that she'd had to deal with it alone, unable to burden him with the enormity of what it meant – that someone else had had to help her because Cal wasn't there.

After Cal was sufficiently satisfied with the pile of wood they'd accumulated, all stacked neatly in the wood store to dry, he went back and forth to the river with the watering can and a bucket, topping up the rainwater tank which now stood empty.

Ida sat and watched him work, knowing that she would do it differently but not wanting to interfere – two buckets worked better, she'd found. They carried more water and, although there was a greater risk of spilling the contents if you slipped, she found the equal weight helped balance her. Cal didn't seem to be having any issues though. He navigated the uneven terrain with ease, barely stopping to take a break. She sat at the top of the hill and watched him work, her eyes never leaving him as he made trip after trip, smiling at her as he passed. At times, she could see he was lost in thought, his mind already moving back beyond the hills, his priorities shifting over to his work. She wanted to pull him back, to hold his focus here with her for longer, but she knew it was futile – she'd tried fighting it many times before and failed.

'You're slacking!' she joked, trying to lighten the mood. An atmosphere had settled between them, charged with dread and uncertainty. It made the air tighter somehow, less easy to breathe.

Cal laughed but it didn't reach his eyes. 'This should do it,' he said, the watering can and the old grey bucket slopping water as he put them down at the peak of the hill. 'It'll be full after these two. Try to keep it topped up, just in case.'

'I will,' she said, knowing that she probably wouldn't, especially since the accident. She took her time walking down to the river now – less nimble, more cautious – watching her step as memories flooded her mind; it made keeping on top of the water supply all the more difficult so she'd begun to let it slide, fetching only what she needed each day. She stretched her bare legs out in front of her. She was wearing her shorts, the spring sunshine full of warmth. Cal stood looking at the house, his chest glistening with sweat. He wiped his forehead with the back of his hand then turned to look at Ida.

'Your go-bag packed?' he asked, his tone suddenly serious.

Ida nodded.

'In the compost bin?'

'Same place as always.'

It was the same conversation every time – a quick run-through of what she would do if trouble came looking for her. Ida knew what she'd do, and Cal knew Ida knew, but it made him feel better to go over it before he left. So Ida let him go through the motions, nodding in all the right places and reassuring him that she knew the plan.

'The guy with the dog...' Cal said, scratching at his beard. 'If he comes, treat him just like anyone else, okay? Just because he's living in solitary doesn't mean he's safe.'

'Okay.'

'You take the go-bag and head to the forest. Camp in the spot we found, okay?' Ida nodded again. 'Watch the house for a few days, make sure he's gone before you come back.'

'You think he'll come looking for supplies?'

Cal shook his head. 'I don't think so, but it's best to be prepared.'

Ida stood up and moved closer to him, putting her hands on his shoulders and resting her head on his chest. She was waiting for him to leave her, and he was waiting for her to say she was ready. Sometimes one came before the other; sometimes they both came at the same time.

Cal kissed the top of Ida's head, firm and unhurried – this was it, this was the goodbye she'd been dreading. 'I have to go, baby,' he whispered.

Ida looked up into his eyes, her own damp with the tears she was clinging on to. She cursed herself for not being the one to tell him to go. She felt conflicted: she knew that Cal leaving represented nothing to do with their relationship – it didn't mean he loved her any less or wanted to be anywhere else but with her – yet sometimes she couldn't help but feel that it did. Before they moved to this place, fleeing the catastrophe that was unfolding back home, being continuously left alone by the man that she loved would have rung alarm bells. Sometimes it was as though Ida's emotions hadn't caught up with the new world and her internal alarm still rang every time he left her; it was in those moments that she craved some control. *Next time*, she thought, *I will be the one to let go first.*

She took a deep breath. 'I know.' She reached up and took his face in her hands, kissing him hard on the lips. Then, before her strength crumbled, she took a step back and put her hands in her pockets. 'Go,' she said.

'I'll miss you every day.'

She didn't respond. She wanted Cal to have the last word, to not taint her memory of his voice with the sound of her own. She watched him walk towards the house where his rucksack was waiting by the door, packed and ready to go; she watched him pull his T-shirt over his head and then the locket with the picture of her nestled inside. He slipped his bag onto his back and looked at her. 'Bye, baby.'

Ida wouldn't watch him walk away. She couldn't. Instead, she turned towards the river and watched the water trickling through the valley; one lifeline in front of her while her other moved further and further away.

CHAPTER NINE

Ida lay on the crest of the hill, her back flat against the grass. She didn't know how long she'd been lying there for, listening to the water rushing past and the birds singing, watching the sky and refusing to acknowledge the beginning of a new period of solitude. Overhead, she saw the distant contrails of an aeroplane. She wondered how high it was flying – thirty thousand feet, maybe, or thirty-five? She liked watching them, it was like a window into the past, a tiny piece of normality. She would lie on her back during the summer months and try to spot the planes as they cruised over on their way to wherever it was they were going. In her mind, she made up stories about them – the people on board or the tropical islands they were visiting. All that adventure and excitement, fictional but comforting.

In reality, they were all ghost flights – containing either no passengers at all or running at ten per cent capacity or less. Cal had told her about them; repatriation flights, sometimes, but mostly political or military. Ida didn't want to hear that the planes she fantasised about actually contained military personnel or politicians on their way to futile talks with other politicians in some faraway location. She wondered how it was possible – or fair – that even in such catastrophic circumstances, the politicians still found a way to survive.

She sat up and arched her back, twisting and bending until she heard it crack; it bothered her more since her fall, the tightness and the stiffness sometimes driving her to take painkillers. She didn't like to use them unless she was desperate, she only had a limited supply and the thought of them tucked away inside her wardrobe made her feel as though she had a safety net.

She looked over at the house, the stone walls and the brick chimney. It couldn't be more than 150 square feet in total, tiny in comparison to the home she'd had before, yet it felt far too big for her every time he left. She didn't look forward to going back inside but she had to, she had a ritual to complete, one she completed every time he left: she would go through the cupboards and take out everything he'd brought, examining each tin or bag or packet in a way she had no interest in while Cal was there. Then she'd put everything back in order – not alphabetically or according to expiration date – if there was one – but an order that made sense to her: The things she wasn't bothered about stayed at the front to be consumed first. The things that would give her something to look forward to were placed at the back. Everything else went in between.

There was also a duplicate bag of food which had gone straight into storage in the little bathroom they'd never really used; the tiny square room with a shower, sink and toilet. There was no running water in the house – there hadn't been for years according to Cal – and the compostable toilet which they'd utilised initially hadn't been used in a long time, the resources and energy it took proving too much. She stored food and an emergency supply of water in there, along with a few other essentials – basic first aid and hygiene supplies. It's also where she kept her backup heater and the matches and firelighters. It was cramped now but it was surprising how quickly the contents could dwindle.

Storage was an ongoing issue in the house. It wasn't that she needed a lot day to day, but once Cal had brought fresh supplies the place seemed crowded, the cupboards overflowing and the shelves crammed. She'd grown used to minimalist living, so a sudden influx of things to store made her feel suffocated. Ida had come to see it as a physical manifestation of Cal's absence; it was only when the cupboards were bare that Cal would reappear.

The temperature was lower inside than it was out on a day like today, the coolness from the night clinging to the stone walls the way that it always did. She grabbed her jumper off the back of the chair and pulled it on, stretching her back and sitting down on the wooden floor. She opened the cupboard; the contents were stacked haphazardly, put away in a rush and left for Ida to organise once Cal had gone.

When she'd first been left alone she'd wondered how she would ever fill the time. She'd imagined long periods of solitude spent staring at the walls and days and nights becoming blurred, her internal clock no longer in tune with a life she couldn't fill. But that hadn't happened. She missed Cal so much that sometimes the physical ache of longing consumed her; out in the meadows, surrounded by empty space, she would fall to her knees and sob, the wind drying her tears until she felt the release she'd been looking for. She never did this in the house; her cries would become trapped there, confined to the four walls and ready to taint the days ahead. But other than those moments of torment and the constant dull ache of missing someone she loved, she got on with things, going about her day and using the coping mechanisms she'd put in place early on.

She spent the better months outdoors in the fresh air, gardening and tending to the land, watching the wildlife and appreciating nature in a way she'd never had time to before. She walked the perimeter to get her exercise or sometimes explored beyond, her bag packed and her mind free. She planted seeds and paddled in the river; she picked wildflowers and arranged them in an empty jam jar on the wooden mantelpiece; she stargazed and listened to the familiar sounds of the animals.

In the colder months she found it harder, but she'd adapted. She spent her time completing jigsaws and doing sudoku puzzles and word searches to keep her brain sharp. She read and reread the books she had stacked on her shelf, curled up in front of the fire. Every evening before bed she tried to solve a Rubik's cube Cal had brought her a couple of years before. She'd grown frustratingly close on a few occasions but, the truth was, she was glad she hadn't completed it – she wasn't ready yet. Like with most things in her life now, she was in no rush. She took her time with things, and the result was that her mind had slowed down along with the new pace of her life. Her body clock adapted to the seasons, waking and sleeping to her own schedule, governed by nature and biology rather than her plans.

She set the food out across the small space between the kitchen cupboards and the little table by the wall. There was a lot; she'd had to stack it and keep moving everything further back. There was a large Tupperware box labelled 'instant mashed potato'. She'd had one of these before. She'd made it up using boiling water in a pan. It was grainy and bland so she decided to put it to one side with a tin of sweetcorn – she would eat those this evening and save half for tomorrow.

There were several tins of vegetables and a couple of fruit – pineapple and peaches. She put them straight to the back, relishing the thought of enjoying them on a warm summer evening. She stacked a few tins of chilli and various different soups and pushed those to the back, too, along with the jams and the beans. When everything was back in the cupboard she realised she hadn't unpacked the pasta and the rice – they were in a separate bag which she'd left out of the way, tucked beside the sofa. She fetched it over to the cupboard and began laying the contents out on the floor. There was a large bag of porridge oats and a Tupperware box full of nuts and raisins at the bottom; Cal had left a note stuck to the top of the latter. *Be strong, baby. No matter when you read this, I'll be thinking of you. Always.*

Ida smiled. Sometimes it was the little things that made her feel special from across the miles. Last year, he'd brought her a book – *A Thousand Splendid Suns* by Khaled Hosseini. Between each chapter, Cal had left her a note; some short, others longer, some simply read *I love you* or *I miss you*. After reading and rereading each little letter, she slipped them back between the pages in their rightful place, knowing that the next time she picked up that book she would have the pleasure of rereading his words all over again.

The Christmas before last, she'd found a present under her pillow. It was small and neatly wrapped in brown paper. She opened it to find a notebook. At the top of each page, he'd written the date – a home-made diary, of sorts, with information that would be important to her. The moons; when she should begin to plant her seeds; the dawn chorus; their anniversary; the beginning of spring. On random days throughout, he'd wrote to her. She hadn't rushed through it, she'd allowed herself one day at a time, always hoping that today would bring more than a blank page. On Valentine's Day, he'd drawn a caricature of the two of them standing on top of the earth together. Underneath he'd written: *When we're together, I'm on top of the world.* She'd laughed, then she'd gone outside and cried, then she'd held it close to her heart and fell asleep with it there.

Ida knew that she would have to go through the inevitable withdrawal as she always did, the sadness and the empty, hollow feeling. She would have to wait until being alone had become her normal again. She hated it; even after all this time she still had to go through this process. She had to let the memories soften – memories of what it felt like to be able to weaken, just a little, while Cal was there to catch her should she fall; to be able to lower her guard ever so slightly, knowing that he had her back.

She took a deep calming breath, pocketed the note, and returned to putting away the supplies.

CHAPTER TEN

The water was ice cold. She'd put the food neatly away in the cupboards then wandered outside searching for something to take her mind off the internal pain – something external and physical. She sat with her feet dipped in the shallow area feeling her skin stinging and her toes turning numb.

Three years earlier, she'd helped Cal drag rocks to create stepping stones in this part of the river. She didn't use them very often, she preferred to paddle through the water on her way to and from the forest, feeling the gravelly bottom of the river against the soles of her feet, but occasionally they proved useful. She had to be careful not to slip on them in the winter; some were jagged and rough, others smooth and potentially hazardous when covered in a thin layer of frost.

Back in January, when the snow had begun to melt, still covering the fields but exposing the taller undergrowth, she'd made her first trip to the forest in search of wood. She'd walked down to the river and seen shards of ice, smooth like glass, being carried along by the water. Already shivering from the cold, she'd decided to keep her shoes on and tentatively cross the stones she knew would be perilous, unable to bring herself to take off her socks and roll up her trousers.

On the last rock she'd slipped and fallen hard. It was as though she'd stepped onto pure ice. Luckily, she'd landed on the other side of the river, one leg in the water but the rest of her on the snow-covered grass. She'd looked back at the stones and then to the water, her heart hammering against her chest as the adrenaline pumped through her body. She knew how close she'd come to tragedy, all alone in the middle of nowhere with no one to see her fall or hear her cries; only now that she thought about it, her feet still dipped in the water, her beliefs about that day had altered. She wasn't alone – at least not as completely as she'd once assumed.

She pushed all thoughts of the man in the hut out of her mind, knowing she was only trying to distract herself from thinking about Cal, from pining for him. He was her rock. He'd saved her. He'd found them somewhere safe to go to before they'd become trapped in a disintegrating world. She tried to remember the day it all happened but she'd blocked so much of the early days out that she struggled to recall the details – just flashes of things she wished she could pluck from her mind and burn to the ground.

Living reclusively had been difficult at first; such isolation can feel particularly cruel and uncomfortable when the change is so drastic and relentless. They'd camped before, they'd been on weekend getaways to isolated spots in the Peak District and the Scottish Highlands, and they'd even wild camped after climbing Snowdon. The difference was the unrelenting nature of what she was being faced with, the consistent absence of everything. She'd struggled with the silence, the lack of facts and data, and the lack of understanding. There was no end point, and it took her a long time to make her peace with that.

She'd spent many nights lying awake feeling suffocated by

the darkness, staring into it and hoping that her other senses would make up for the depletion of another. She felt as though she were on the lookout for invisible fires everywhere, trying to guess where they would pop up but knowing she would be unable to extinguish them if they did. They would just grow in intensity, the fury of the flames burning everything to the ground. She could almost feel their heat – impossible yet so very real in the depths of the night.

They'd found the house via a remote rentals company on the internet and paid for it three months up front, using up a big chunk of their savings. When they were nearing the end of the three months, it was Cal who'd ventured back to civilisation to find out what was left; to find out whether it was safe for them to return to their little house in Surrey. He was away for almost two weeks – twelve days of Ida being completely alone for the first time in her life. She felt it in everything she did, the acute absence of Cal and everything she was used to.

She cried herself to sleep at night, her desperation and isolation combining and festering like a disease. She felt physically ill, the monumental weight of it too much to bear. She'd begun to think he wasn't coming back, that he'd perished along with the rest of the world. She'd convinced herself that she was the only person left on the planet.

On the tenth day of Cal's absence, she'd ventured outside and lay down on the grass. The clouds parted to reveal a patch of bright blue sky and she saw something that gave her a little spark of hope: a plane. The ghost flights had always reminded her that, even when she felt it, she wasn't alone.

'We don't need to worry about the house,' Cal had said when he returned. 'We can stay as long as we want.'

'What... what do you mean?' He hadn't responded straight away and Ida had stepped closer to him, searching for eye contact, trying to anchor him. 'Cal? You're scaring me.'

'People aren't bothered about money anymore. There aren't many...' He'd taken a deep, steadying breath. 'There aren't many left.'

'Many what?'

'People,' he'd whispered.

Ida had panicked then and Cal had held her. Her knees buckled and Cal had lowered her to the ground and wrapped a blanket around her shoulders, despite knowing her shaking was nothing to do with the cold.

Later on, cradling a cup of sweet tea in her hands, she'd asked him to tell her everything, to tell her what had happened while they'd been hidden away. They both knew that she didn't really want to hear *everything*, but she needed to ask. So Cal gave her a summary, telling her what she needed to know and leaving out what she didn't.

'The Cabinet Office failed to keep control. From what I could make out, there's not really a government, so to speak, just a handful of politicians who've formed a board, and then the army who have control. There's no power, no phone network. Nothing. Martial law was declared a few weeks after we left. They're trying to set up safe zones but...'

'But what?'

'It's a mess, Ida. It's chaos. Utter chaos.' He shook his head. 'It's not safe.'

'What about Maeve and the girls? Did you find them?'

'No, but I will. I promise I will.'

'You're going back?' She could hear the panic in her voice and feel it in her veins, the sudden surge of frantic energy that had made her rise to her feet. 'You can't leave me here again. You can't!'

'They need more people. More manpower.'

'No. No, Cal. No, no, no...'

It was the promise of finding the ones they'd left behind that made Ida accept the unimaginable in the end. The thought of him leaving made her physically unwell. Twice she was sick and on several occasions her panic took over, sending her spiralling into a pit of despair. She felt as though he was abandoning her, leaving her for the land to consume.

'Ida, I'm doing this for you. For us.'

'No! No you're not! This has nothing to do with me!' She'd shouted the words through panicked breaths and uncontrollable tears, crying so much that her head pounded and snot ran down her chin. She'd wiped it away with the sleeve of her jumper and thrown herself onto the bed, holding on to her pillow and sobbing into it, trying to release the pain that would not leave her.

Cal had sat down beside her and stroked her hair. 'I'll find Maeve and the girls.'

Ida had turned to look at him, her eyes red and swollen, her hair stuck to the sad streaks of tears which ran down her cheeks. 'What if they're not there to find?'

'We have to have hope, Ida. We have to keep believing that the ones we love have found a way to survive, just like we have.'

'They're not like you.'

Cal lay down on the bed beside her and took her hand. 'Like *us*,' he'd corrected her.

'No. No.' She'd shook her head rigorously but Cal stopped her by taking hold of her chin.

'Yes. Like *us*. You're strong, Ida. Stronger than you realise right now because you have me to lean on. It's amazing what we're capable of when we don't have a choice.'

'Let me come with you,' she'd pleaded. 'I can help.'

'No.' His voice had been firm. Authoritative. 'I need to

know you're safe or I won't be able to function, Ida. You're the most important thing in my life and you're helping by staying here. By keeping safe. By giving me something to fight for. Something to return to.'

'I won't be able to do it without you!'

'Yes. Yes you will.' He'd kissed her and held her and told her how much he loved her; how proud he was of her. Ida had held him tighter than she thought possible, never wanting to let him go but knowing that she would have to.

Ida had thought of her sister and her twin girls. She missed their innocence. It had been a long time since she'd seen Maeve, even before she went away, but she'd never stopped thinking about her; never stopped loving her. Fresh tears began to fall as she tried to picture her nieces' little faces and their long red hair, just like hers – but she couldn't. All she saw was an empty house, their swing set unused and the wildflowers left to wilt and die. She couldn't *feel* them anymore, and her heart ached because of it. She couldn't take the uncertainty.

'You'll find them?' she'd asked.

'I'll find them.' Cal had taken her hand in his and brought it to his mouth, kissing it over and over again.

'You promise?'

'I promise.'

CHAPTER ELEVEN

The wind hissed through the fields, the grassland coarse and overgrown. The sky had turned overnight from the crystal blues of the day before to the dull greys which now blocked out the sun. It never failed to surprise Ida how much the weather could impact her mood, as though the greyness penetrated her skin and poisoned her mind. The land responded too, the wildflowers sad and drooping, no golden sunlight for them to reach for.

Ida sighed and pulled her robe closer to her while she waited for the water to boil, looking out of the window and across the vast expanse of green. It was grey and dreary, the sky threatening rain, the whole place sitting in shadow, but it still looked quite beautiful – wild and full of wonder; nature thriving where people were unable to. Ida watched a bird out on the lawn, a long-tailed tit, tiny with a snowy white belly and black-and-pink wings. It rummaged through the grass looking for food, then with a beak full of something Ida couldn't make out, it flew off into the undergrowth.

She'd become quite the birdwatcher since living here. The house had been all but empty when they'd arrived, just a couple of blankets in the wardrobe and basic kitchen utensils in the cupboards. But on top of the wooden mantel above the fireplace were a stack of books that had proven to be one of Ida's most prized possessions – along with the old jigsaw puzzles and game of Scrabble they'd found in the bedroom cupboard. The books ranged from birdwatching to gardening to bushcraft and foraging and they had helped her both physically and mentally over the years.

The water began to bubble and she lowered the heat, pouring half of the pan into her mug and leaving half sat on the kitchen worktop. She watched as the teabag bled into the water – raspberry and pomegranate this time; different with every supply and none of them comparable to the sweet, milky tea Ida had loved before. She'd been down to the river early, the darkness of the night still tinging the skies. Something had woke her, though she couldn't put her finger on what. She'd looked out of the window in the bedroom and then the one in the kitchen, but there was nothing to see except the night staring back at her, so absolute that it was as though the outside world no longer existed, the darkness having taken everything.

When she'd failed to see anything to account for her sudden alertness, she'd lay in bed listening instead, wondering what it was that had stirred her from sleep so early. She used to wake that way every morning when they'd first arrived, and at regular intervals throughout the night, thrust from dreams she couldn't recall. It was the kind of fear she couldn't remember ever feeling before. Cal would put his arm around her and pull her into him, holding her close.

'I'm scared,' she'd whisper.

'Nothing to be scared of here, baby. We're safe,' he'd soothe, his eyes remaining closed, teetering on the cusp of sleep.

Ida would nestle into him, the hairs on his chest tickling her forehead. She would listen to him sleeping – his long, steady breaths and the occasional flutter of movement – until the sunlight streaked in through the gap in the curtains, the crimson light leaking into the inky sky that had seemed so harsh and punishing just moments before. She would lie waiting for that light, for the sunrise that would reassure her that the day was on its way, then she would fall asleep to the warmth of it filling the room, chasing her fears away.

Ida sat at the little wooden table and drank her tea, a jigsaw set out in front of her, the outline complete but the centre pieces scattered in no particular order. She began sorting them into colours. It had been six weeks since Cal had left and so far nothing noteworthy had happened. The vegetable garden was coming along nicely; the first of the lettuces were ready to be picked and the carrots, tomatoes and potatoes were thriving. She'd planted another round of seeds already and was going to begin the final wave this week, hopefully extending the harvest period into the autumn. But she was, as always, at the mercy of Mother Nature, and the grey skies outside today told her they were expecting some inclement conditions.

She decided that today was an indoor day, apart from another water run and a quick venture out to the vegetable plot to pick some lettuce leaves. She was going to open a tin of chilli and mix in some rice and use the lettuce as wraps; her tummy rumbled at the thought of it, but for now she would have to make do with her mug of tea and a handful of nuts and raisins.

Occasionally she would allow herself to fantasise about the things she missed, but not very often. She found the safest thing to daydream about was food – vanilla lattes from her local coffee shop; hot buttered toast; cheese and pickle sandwiches; apple pie, warm with ice cream; a can of cold Coke... Every now and then she would be overcome by a sudden craving, a pang so intense it was all she could think about, but it didn't happen very often anymore. Most recently, she couldn't stop thinking about chocolate, cold and fresh out of the fridge. She'd imagined it melting on her tongue and she'd felt her mouth watering in expectation.

Sometimes, when Cal brought her something special, she would have to fight the urge to tell him to take it away. She didn't want to seem ungrateful but she knew only too well that it was often worse to have a little bit of something than nothing at all; the former makes you feel deprived while the latter makes you feel in control – however false and insignificant that control may be.

Ida stood the jigsaw lid up on the table so she could see the picture. It was one of her favourites – a volcano erupting in the distance while waves from the surrounding sea crashed against black rocks in the foreground. She liked the contrasting colours, the way the reds and oranges of the lava streaked into the night sky. It reminded her of sunrise, and it reminded her of Cal and the first weeks they'd shared together in the house.

'Look what I've found.' He'd walked barefoot out of the bedroom wearing his boxer shorts and a grey T-shirt. He was carrying several boxes in his hands, all with tattered edges or collapsing sides. He'd put them down on the table where Ida was sat cradling her knees to her chest, her fingers interlocked and her eyes casting scornful looks through the window, out over the bleak landscape. It was warm but dull, the rain stop-starting and the sun barely getting a look-in. 'Guess what I found? Scrabble!' Cal held the box out to her and she looked at it and smiled thinly. 'No? Okay, what about a jigsaw? We've got a forest, a beach or hot air balloons. Oh, or a volcano.'

Ida had looked at the box and the picture which glared back at her, the rage of the volcano like a mirror. 'The volcano,' she'd said.

'Good choice.' Cal had smiled, undoing the box and

emptying out the contents, scattering the pieces across the table with his hands.

They'd sat and completed the whole thing, all one thousand pieces. Cal had sorted through the pile looking for the corners while telling her about Mount Tambora in Indonesia, and the devastation caused by its eruption in the nineteenth century. When he'd finished talking, he'd looked at Ida and suddenly seemed to realise the macabre turn in conversation. Cal was one of those people who knew a little bit about a lot; you could ask him about anything and he'd be able to tell you something. It was one of the things she loved about him – his appetite for knowledge – and even then, discussing the death of thousands of people, she could still appreciate his intent: he wanted to fill her head with useless information that would distract her from reality. She'd just wished that it would have been a different kind of useless information, less depressing and more benign; one that didn't remind her so painfully of their reality.

He'd taken her hand across the table and stroked the back of it with his thumb. 'Life is what we make it here, Ida.'

'It just seems so... so...' She couldn't find the right word, but Cal waited patiently, allowing her the time she needed. 'Overwhelming,' she settled on.

'I know it does, baby. I know.'

'Don't you feel it?' Ida asked. She didn't think that he did; he seemed content. He didn't have the same sense of loss that she felt so deeply, or maybe he just didn't show it. He'd always been happy when it was just the two of them, even when they'd first started dating. His tendency to want to strip back the chaos and relax in their own company had rubbed off on her to some degree, allowing her to take the time to enjoy things rather than rushing to make everything fit. But this... this wasn't taking time, it was basking in it; it was removing everything else entirely so that all they had was *time*.

'Feel what?'

'Overwhelmed.'

'Overwhelmed?' Cal had shrugged, frowning slightly.

'Yes, with the situation. With leaving everything behind.'

'Sometimes.'

'Only sometimes?'

'It's not going to be easy, Ida, but we're together. Anything else is a bonus, right?'

'But what about our families, Cal? What about my sister and my nieces? What about our friends...' Her eyes had begun to fill with tears again at the mention of the ones she'd left behind. Cal's eyes closed momentarily as though gathering himself to once again discuss the crux of all of Ida's worries – the ones they couldn't bring with them, the people that haunted her day and night.

'Ida, listen to me: your sister would have wanted you to have the best possible chance. And once things have settled down, I will go back and I will find her and the girls.'

'But I want to come with you. I want to find them.'

'I need to protect you, Ida. *You* are my priority. Let me take care of you, okay?'

Ida nodded.

'I'll find them. I promise you.'

She'd got up from her chair and sat down on Cal's knee, her arms wrapped around his shoulders. 'I know you will.' She'd kissed him, and he'd kissed her back, the jigsaw puzzle spread out on the table behind her. Images of Maeve had floated around her head, and then her nieces and her friends, all of them suspended there, lost in a void of time she was unable to account for.

CHAPTER TWELVE

I da had been having a late afternoon nap. She'd spent most of the day indoors doing her jigsaw and reading her books, cuddled up on the sofa with a patchwork blanket which still smelled of Cal. She'd drifted off halfway through a chapter and fallen head first into dreams of him. She often did this – her memories surfacing during her sleep, the ones she wouldn't allow herself to dwell on during the day. It had never sat right with her that such happy memories could make her so sad, reminiscing in moments she felt so far detached from, knowing she may never get to experience such things again. It felt as though she was tainting the things she held dear, poisoning or diluting her memories with her loneliness and grief, but in her sleep there was no dull ache to accompany them, they existed independent of her conscious mind; protected.

She was walking barefoot on a beach, the rhythmic sounds of the waves accompanying her as they crashed against the rocky shoreline ahead. The air was warm and salty, the sun casting long shadows as she walked. It was busy; children were playing with buckets and spades and bats and balls, rushing in and out of the water as the waves rolled in; couples lay sprawled sparsely clothed, the coconut scent of their suntan lotion tinting the air as Ida zigzagged in and out of the crowds.

When she reached the rocks she sat down beside them, the sand warm against her bare legs. She picked up a shell and held it in her palm – a sea scallop, pink with a white trim at the fanned edges. She placed it down beside her and buried it. The sea was rough and choppy, the waves growing in intensity until they crashed near to the shoreline sending salty splashes into the air behind her. She looked out at the vastness of the ocean, holding her hand up to shield her eyes from the low sun, a light breeze lifting the ends of her hair. There were a couple of jet-skiers bobbing over the waves; she watched as they sped into the distance leaving a spray of water in their wake.

When she looked back to the beach she could see Cal running towards her, shirtless and shoeless, his bare feet kicking up the sand as he struck it. She kept her eyes on him as he moved closer to her, weaving in and out of the crowds. When he reached her he stood to the side, blocking out the sun and plunging her into his shadow. She handed him a bottle of water and he tipped half over his head before drinking the rest.

'Ready for a swim?' He smiled at her but Ida looked away.

He held out his hand to help her up but she didn't take it. She moved her fingers backwards and forwards through the fine grains of sand like a rake, feeling for the pebbles and shells which hid there, distracting herself. He stepped forward and bent down to take her hand in his, pulling her up to her feet with ease. Ida kept her eyes on the ground and her toes in the sand and Cal, understanding her reluctance, wrapped his arms around her and held her close. She suddenly felt very small, her tiny frame dwarfed by his. She could feel the sweat on his chest as she cried, the sun warm on her back as he kissed her head.

'Come on, Ida, let's go for a swim.' He undid the black lacy sarong which was tied around her waist, letting it fall to the sand to reveal her green swimming costume. Her red hair hung loose over her shoulders, wild and untamed, like the waves which greeted them.

Something woke her, a noise so sudden and piercing that it cut straight through her sleep, an abrupt end to her dreams which left Ida confused. One minute she was with Cal, standing on a warm beach surrounded by crowds of people; the next she was alone, her heart thumping and her breathing heavy. She looked first to the door at the front of the house and then to the window above the kitchen sink, but she couldn't see anything but the greyness which still lurked outside, now accompanied by a heavy onslaught of rain. The clouds beyond the river were so thick and low that they almost touched the tops of the trees – Ida didn't think she'd ever seen them look so ominous; so threatening. She ran barefoot into the bedroom and checked the back window, out towards the rolling hills. Nothing.

She knew she'd heard something. She tried frantically to recall what it sounded like but before she'd had a chance to calm her mind and think straight she heard it again: a sudden explosion like a gunshot. The sky lit up with it, bright and consuming, the heavens alive and the patchwork of clouds temporarily illuminated. Ida's first thought was that it was a bomb – an abrupt end to a world that was already in decline. She backed away from the window and her hands found the wooden surface of the table. She gripped it, looking out of the window with wild eyes, fully expecting to see the end of the world progressing ever closer.

But it didn't. Instead, she heard it again, and this time she *saw* it – a huge bolt of lightning over the forest, forking off at odd angles and almost filling the entirety of the sky. It couldn't be more than five hundred metres away. Ida wasn't sure what to do; this wasn't something she'd prepared for or discussed with Cal. She'd dealt with adverse weather conditions many times – snow, heavy rain and floods, strong winds; she'd even endured her fair share of thunderstorms before, but nothing like this. Nothing this *close*.

She looked out of the window waiting for the next strike, willing it to be passing through in any direction but hers. When it came, it was closer – just at the edge of the forest. The lightning seemed to appear rather than shoot down from the sky; one minute there was nothing and the next there was a flash of light running all the way to the ground, right through the middle of a tree. Ida squinted, trying to see better through the rain which had gathered on the window, water splashing and blurring her view. The tree seemed to collapse in on itself, falling to the ground in surrender. Ida gasped, panicking. Thunderstorms had never bothered her before, they'd always felt quite magical, bordering on supernatural – an event to behold, Mother Nature showing her power. But now it was encroaching on her space and her feeling of relative safety in a world which did not feel safe at all.

The rain was lashing against the roof and the wind was howling through the trees – the noise was making it difficult for Ida to think straight. She looked around the room, searching for something but she didn't know what. She thought she could remember reading somewhere that you should crouch down low in a thunderstorm, touching as little of the ground as possible. She couldn't exactly call it a plan but it was all she had. She squatted down low to the floor next to the table and crouched into a ball, her head tucked in and her feet holding her weight. She swayed awkwardly, her thighs cramping as she tensed.

Moments later there was a deafening blast that made Ida lose her balance; she fell backwards and felt something hit her shoulder as she lay huddled to one side, her knees drawn up to her chest. Her eyes were closed tight and her jaw tense. She held her shoulder as it throbbed, the sound of gushing wind filling her ears. She heard the intermittent sound of things smashing against the wooden floors around her. She lay like that for a long time, until her hip ached from the pressure of holding her weight and her hair was wet from the rain. Only then did she slowly open her eyes and sit up, taking in the damage around her.

She could smell something sweet and fresh mixed with the distinctive tang of smoke. She looked up at the roof and saw a patch of the sky, grey and overcast, the rain falling through the gaping hole in the roof and landing among the broken tiles now littering the floor around her, some of them singed at the edges.

The rain was unrelenting, it poured in without mercy, filling the house and soaking all of its contents. Ida didn't know what to do, there was too much – too many things that required her attention. She couldn't think straight.

Her hair stuck to her face, limp and dripping with rainwater, masking the tears which had started to fall. It didn't matter anymore, she thought; they couldn't become trapped here, nothing could. She looked up to the hole in the ceiling and the teetering slate tiles which sat ominously around it, wondering how on earth she had ever felt safe.

CHAPTER THIRTEEN

Ida sat cross-legged on the kitchen worktop, her back slumped against the wall and her robe pulled tightly around her. Her hair was damp from the rain and her body fatigued from the stress. She'd pulled the blanket off her bed and covered herself with it, trying to keep warm as the night descended on her. She hadn't dared to go to bed despite the exhaustion that had set in long ago, the darkness sweeping in through the open roof and filling her space with the threat of the unknown.

She'd lit two candles and left them burning on the kitchen table, casting a flicker of light on the wall. She watched it move with the wind which still whipped through the house, calmer but still angry, looking for places to fill. The coolness it brought lingered in the stone walls and crept under Ida's skin; she shivered, her list of sounds gripped tightly in her hands, the words unreadable in the dim light cast by the flames.

The mild days had fooled her and she'd become complacent, enjoying the comfort and the freedom that the warmer climate afforded her. She hadn't considered that it was a temporary reprieve, an anomaly which would soon be turned upside down. She shouldn't have been so naïve, she should have protected herself mentally and been prepared for a sudden change and the impact this would have on her. The storm had seen to it that she would never again be able to enjoy the luxury of warm weather without looking over her shoulder and up to the sky.

Ida adjusted her weight, her back tight and uncomfortable against the hard stone wall. The truth was, she didn't dare to go to bed because she didn't want to fall asleep; the house didn't feel safe anymore. The reality of her already precarious existence had come crashing down around her, angry and raw, and it had reminded her of the horrors which lurked around the corner, the chaos she had so far avoided. Maybe this was her comeuppance, nature delivering her fair share and reminding her that nowhere was safe; no one was untouchable. Ida knew it wasn't personal – it couldn't be, it was just a random act of nature – but still, she couldn't help feeling that somehow, it was. All that land, all that empty space, and the heavens unleashed their fury on *her* house; *her* sanctuary. It certainly *felt* personal.

She thought of Cal, wondering whether there was any way he would know what had happened. Would he *feel* it? Would he sense her distress? Would something tell him that she needed help? She wanted so desperately for that to be true, to discover their souls were linked in some inconceivable way that defied logic and science, but she just didn't believe in that kind of thing; soulmates and connections or love at first sight.

She'd tried to believe in a greater force, in some reason for everything happening – a plan by some higher power. She'd tried to believe it was her calling – a caretaker to the remote landscape she'd somehow inherited. On occasion, she'd begun to feel a connection to the land, to hear whispers through the forest or see warnings in the sky, but now, looking at the hole in the roof, she knew she'd been right to be sceptical. There was no higher power and the land didn't protect her; it never would.

She stared up into the sky, the clouds still thick and heavy, masking the blanket of stars which lay beyond. She was in trouble. She sighed heavily and pulled the blanket closer to her. It was going to be a long night.

When morning came, it was glorious. The air was fresh and sweet, scented by the storm, and the rain had stopped. A collage of clouds remained high and scattered in the sky, tinged pink and purple by the glow of the low sun. Ida stood on the step outside her house with the blanket wrapped around her shoulders. She couldn't believe her own memories, the sky and the land showed no recollection of the storm – except for the jagged spike of the tree which remained on the outskirts of the forest, and the rest of it which lay strewn in bits.

She turned back to face the inside of her house, the waterlogged floors and the rain which clung to everything she owned; the hole in the roof which left her vulnerable in ways she could not yet fully appreciate, her mind too muddled, her spirit broken. The threat was there; the realisation teetering on the cusp of her consciousness, ready to flood her with fear. If she turned back to face the north or the east, she could pretend nothing had happened. So that's what she did. She stood watching the sun rise like a fire igniting on the horizon, the start of a new day she didn't want to come. She became lost in it, her mind drifting to Cal, wondering whether he was watching it too. She hoped that wherever he was, he was accompanied by better circumstances. She turned to the north, watching the damp grass blowing in the morning wind, teasing herself with memories of Cal walking towards her, a backpack slung over his shoulders and a smile on his face.

As the sun rose into the sky and began to warm Ida's face,

she stepped out onto the grass in bare feet – her boots were filled with rain and wouldn't be dry for some time, as were most of her clothes. She did a lap of the house, looking for further damage she hoped she wouldn't find. She held her breath as she rounded the corner to her vegetable patch but was relieved to find it was largely okay – the vegetables had withstood the ferocity of the winds and would hopefully thrive from the abundance of rainwater.

The back of the house was largely unaffected, the slate tiles still in place and her bedroom window in one piece, but her butterfly bush from Cal looked dishevelled, the leaves skewed under the heaviness of the rain. On the other side of the house, where she kept the generator, she noticed a couple of broken tiles had fallen and smashed, jagged pieces scattered among the grass. She stepped over them, towards the generator. It was stood sturdily under the makeshift shelter Cal had attached to the house, but it hadn't protected it fully – it was wet. Ida had expected it, but it still dampened her spirits. She wouldn't be able to use it until it had fully dried, and she had no idea how long that would take so she knew she would have to err on the side of caution, and that would leave her without electricity for a few days, at the very least.

The generator had never been rained on before. Usually, the wooden awning shielded it from the onslaught, but it had managed to find its way in this time, accompanied by the ferocity of the wind. The generator sat atop a few layers of bricks, a makeshift table Cal had set up to keep it off the floor. Looking at the saturated ground now, it was a good job he'd had the foresight or it could have been much worse. Ida sighed heavily. No heating, no hob, no appliances. She would have to use her emergency water supply, she couldn't risk drinking straight from the river despite the apparent cleanliness of the water; Cal had told her that when they'd first arrived – even if the water looked crystal clear it could still be full of bacteria. If she got sick out here, she would be in trouble.

At the front of the house she stepped back to get a better look – the lightning had hit the roof just below the chimney. Most of the tiles had fallen inside but a few lay strewn around the grass. The hole looked to be between two and three feet in diameter – big enough to cause sufficient problems and big enough to cause Ida to panic. Without a proper roof, she would be exposed not only to the elements but the wildlife, too. She would no longer be able to shut herself away and feel safe. Her only saving grace was that it was easing into the warmest months, but even that did little to alleviate her concerns.

She stared up at the roof and the ugly hole which sat there, considering all of her options. Her mind flitted to the basic toolbox Cal had used in the early days to put up the fence and the wood store and shelter. There were some materials left over but nothing that would fill a hole like that. She had a ladder but little know-how. It frustrated her as much as it upset her; it had taken her a long time to feel competent, to feel relatively comfortable on her own, and all it took was one bad storm to strip away her independence and leave her longing for Cal.

The earth beneath her had turned to mud and it clung to her feet and worked its way between her toes, the tall grass tickling her legs. She ran her fingers through her still-damp hair and took some deep breaths, gathering herself, willing herself not to cry; she didn't have the energy to waste on it.

Ida went back into the house and looked around at the water puddling on the floor and the sporadic drips falling from the roof. The sofa and the patchwork blanket were sodden, and a pile of her clothes which she'd folded and placed beside the fireplace were now swimming among the water which gathered there. She looked at her pile of books stacked on the wooden mantel above the fire; they'd avoided taking the brunt of the rain but their edges still curled. Ida felt a pang of anger, knowing that they would never be the same. Perhaps, neither would she.

At a loss as to where to start, she paddled into the bedroom and sat down heavily on the bed – the only dry space left. She was exhausted, drained in a way that left her unable to think clearly. She pulled her legs up to her chest and held them there, feeling her heart drumming against her ribs. She let her mind wander to her little house in Surrey, her sage-green bedding soft against her skin. As she taunted herself with memories she heard something at the window, sharp and sudden. Her eyes darted around the room: there was someone there – the shadow of someone standing behind the glass, their tall frame visible through the thin floral curtains.

CHAPTER FOURTEEN

I da stepped backwards until she bumped into the door, her bare feet slapping against the wet floorboards. Her heart wanted it to be Cal more than anything but her mind knew that it wasn't. Cal wouldn't tap at the window like that, and he wouldn't be back so soon; Ida wouldn't allow herself to start anticipating his arrival for another six weeks at the very least.

There was another tap at the window, a little louder this time. Ida's heart was pummelling in her chest but she kept her breathing steady, hardly daring to make a sound.

'You in there?' came a voice. Seconds later, before she'd had a chance to consider a response, she heard a dog barking.

She thought she recognised the low, gravelly voice as belonging to the man from the hut, but she wasn't sure. She waited, hoping that he'd say more, but he didn't. The shadowy form moved away leaving a narrow strip of sunlight seeping in between the gap in the curtains. She listened, waiting to see whether he would come to the kitchen window or the front door. Her mind quickly tried to recall whether she'd locked it; she had to have, it was a force of habit, yet she found she was questioning herself. She slowly pulled back the bedroom door and walked into the kitchen, looking out of the window towards the forest, but she couldn't see anything.

She checked the front door – it was locked. She pressed her ear against it, feeling the rough wood against her cheek, but all she could hear was the gentle wind. She took a deep breath, unlocked it and opened it just enough to see straight out over the fields. And there he was – walking north with his dog. The man from the hut.

'Hey!' she shouted, not knowing whether it was the right thing to do or not. She'd spent such a long time avoiding people that it felt wrong to reach out, but even Ida knew when her back was up against a wall.

The man heard her shout and turned, looking over to the house and at Ida stood in her robe and bare feet, her hair whipping around her face. She tried in vain to tuck it behind her ears but she soon gave up and held her hand up in the air, tentatively waving over to the man. The gesture felt so strange and unfamiliar; she quickly thought better of it and tucked her hands inside her pockets instead. The man began to walk back towards the house, in no particular hurry, his stick in his hand and his dog at his side. As he drew nearer, Ida began to question herself, to wonder whether she'd done the right thing, shouting over this man she barely knew; a man who could be dangerous in more ways than one. The wind howling through the gap in her roof was the only thing that stopped her acting on the sudden impulse she felt to retreat back inside and slam the door shut.

The man walked until he was stood a couple of metres away from her, then he looked up at the roof and back to Ida before he spoke. 'Quite the storm we had.'

'The lightning hit the roof,' Ida explained.

'I can see that,' said the man. The dog had wandered over to the step Ida was stood on and was sniffing at her dirty feet, still stained with mud. The man looked past her and into the house, but if he was shocked by the state of it his expression didn't give it away.

'The rain...' Ida began. She looked over her shoulder and then stepped to the side, allowing him a clearer view of the house. This was, she realised, her way of asking for help. Not necessarily physical help, and not necessarily emotional; somewhere in between.

'Flooded,' the man acknowledged, nodding. 'You need to secure the roof,' he said. 'Before we get more rain.' He looked up towards the sky as though it could come at any minute.

'I don't... I don't have anything... I need some tarpaulin or... or...' Ida was struggling to string a sentence together, her pride getting in the way of saying I *need help*.

'I've got some tarp.'

'You do?'

The man nodded. 'I'll bring some by.'

'You don't need to do that.'

'I know that,' he said flatly, as though it were the most obvious thing in the world. 'What about the flood?' the man asked her.

'Well I... I need to get the water out.'

Another nod. 'Scoop up what you can. The rest will dry in time.' He shrugged.

'Your place... is it okay?'

'My place is fine.' He scratched his head and looked over his shoulder, his gaze lingering on the distant horizon for a moment before turning back to Ida. 'I saw the lightning over yours. I didn't think you'd mind me ignoring the signs to check you were alive.'

'Oh... no, not at all.' Ida thought of the handmade signs she'd put up with Cal. *Keep out! Private property! No trespassing!*

The man nodded and turned to leave, taking a few steps before turning back. 'You got tools?' he asked.

'Tools?'

'Yeah, hammer, nails...'

'Oh, yes, I think so.' Ida's mind drifted to the red metal toolbox she kept in the old bathroom, on top of the window ledge. It was well stocked, but she'd never had much use for it before.

'Ladder?'

Ida nodded. 'Yes, I have a ladder.'

'I'll just bring the tarp then.' He turned round again and whistled, his dog's ears pricking as he scurried to his side. Ida watched them go, stood on the step of her flooded house, a mixture of emotions flooding her mind. It felt so unnatural to accept help from someone other than Cal that it filled her with a sense of foreboding; but at the same time, she was grateful to this stranger, for offering her an olive branch when she so desperately needed one.

She didn't bother closing the door, she knew she'd be in and out for a good while. She grabbed one of the buckets and placed it on the step, then she took Cal's camper van mug out of the cupboard and began scooping up the water. It wasn't easy, the water was at a frustrating level of being too deep to leave it but just shallow enough to make it difficult to collect. She used her hand to fan it into the mug, then tipped what she'd managed to get into the bucket outside. Her back ached from the bending and the crouching and the hem of her robe was dripping wet. But still she carried on, not stopping or slowing, determined to help herself before accepting the help of the man.

An hour or so later she could finally see visual improvements. The floorboards were saturated with the water that had seeped through them but little remained flowing on top. She was worried about the wood rotting or mould growing, but there was little she could do about that right now. She had to let them dry. She opened the kitchen window and then the one in her bedroom, leaving the internal door propped open using a chair to allow the wind to blow through.

She gathered her books and took them outside, setting them atop of the wood store to dry off in the sun. Then she traipsed round the house and collected anything she could hang out to dry – the patchwork quilt, her clothes and both pairs of her boots. She pegged them all out on the line to the south of the house, running just in front of her butterfly bush. As she finished, she saw a beautiful holly blue land on one of the branches, its silver-blue wings fluttering in the warmth of the sun. Ida watched it for a moment, enjoying the simple pleasure of nature and reminded herself it wasn't her enemy.

'Hello?' she heard the man's deep, raspy voice coming from the other side of the house; it disturbed the butterfly which flew off towards the hills.

Ida walked round the western side of the house, collecting the generator as she did. Waiting at the front was the man and his dog, a huge sheet of blue tarpaulin rolled up under his arm, his trusty stick in the other. He looked at the generator in Ida's hand and frowned. 'Broke?' he asked.

Ida shrugged. 'Wet.' The man nodded but didn't appear to have anything to add, so Ida dragged it round to the wood store and left it in the light of the sun. 'I'll get the ladder.' She walked back round to the wooden awning and collected the metal ladder which leaned against the wall under it. When she emerged back to the front of the house she noticed the man was looking inside, his dog sat beside him.

'Looking better,' he commented.

'I got out what I could.'

The man put the tarpaulin down on the grass and took the ladder from her.

'Do you need any help?' Ida asked.

'Just a toolbox.'

Ida went back inside and retrieved it from the bathroom, feeling its weight in her hands as she did. 'There should be everything you need in there.'

The man had leaned the ladder against the roof in the direction of the hole. He took the toolbox from her and set it on the floor, kneeling down on the wet grass as he opened it. He took out a hammer and a handful of nails which he stuffed into a pocket on the side of his cargo shorts.

'Right,' he said, 'I'll get to it.'

Ida watched him climb the ladder, his shabby old hiking boots frayed at the laces and his bare legs tanned and weathered. She wanted to shout and tell him thank you, that she appreciated his help, but she couldn't quite bring herself to say it. It felt as though it would be handing over some of her power – or the illusion of – or admitting that she *needed* his help. So instead she stood and watched as he unrolled the tarp and spread it out over the hole, appearing to need nothing from Ida but the hammer in his hand and the nails in his pocket.

CHAPTER FIFTEEN

I da stood feeling like a spare part and it irked her. She was used to taking the lead and tending to her own house and land, taking a back seat only to Cal when he visited. It felt odd watching a man she barely knew – whose name she didn't even know – climb up onto her roof and begin hammering nails into it. She wasn't sure whether she should stand there watching him, waiting to see whether she was needed, or whether she should leave him to it.

For some reason, a memory surfaced from her life before – a dinner party at the home they'd recently moved into, hosting Cal's friends and their partners. Ida had felt uncomfortable, constantly questioning the way she was acting or the things she was saying. Cal had told her not to worry, that his friends liked her, but she never really got that impression herself. She'd cooked a pasta dish only to discover that one of their guests had a gluten allergy. Cal had squeezed her hand as the woman had helped herself to a large portion of salad, saying quietly: 'I told you Verity was gluten free.' She'd spent the rest of the evening feeling as though she'd done something wrong, even though she was quite sure that she hadn't – she would have remembered something like that, she was sure of it.

Ida couldn't put her finger on why this memory sprung to mind at first, it seemed like an odd thing to think about given the circumstances, but then she realised: it was the crippling self-doubt. She wasn't sure if she was doing the right thing, allowing this man to gain insight into her home, to arm himself with the knowledge of the layout of the house and the things she kept inside. She wasn't sure what Cal would say about it, the same way she wasn't sure what Cal was going to say after his friends had left and the plates were cleared away.

She decided to go back inside and make herself useful. The house smelled damp and musty and she could hear the rhythmic pounding of the nails being hammered into the roof as he worked above her. She looked up and saw the sheet of blue now blocking out the sky.

She looked around the room trying to decide where to start. The sofa, she decided. She pulled the seating cushions off and hauled them outside, water dripping from them as she carried them, one under each arm. She was suddenly conscious that her shoulder was throbbing from where one of the roof slates had fallen on her. She lined the cushions against the outer wall of the house hoping that the sun would dry them but knowing it would take more than a day. When she was back inside she pulled her robe down over her shoulder and saw a long linear bruise beginning to form across it, her skin angry and red around it.

'You hurt?' The man was in her doorway, appearing as though from nowhere.

Ida turned away from him and quickly pulled her robe back over her shoulder, adjusting it tight around her waist.

'Sorry,' he said, 'didn't mean to intrude.' He was holding the toolbox in his hands with the hammer balanced on top; he put it down beside the door.

'One of the slates fell on me,' she said.

'Cut?'

Ida shook her head. 'Just bruised.'

'How's your head?' Ida had forgot all about the cut on her head and the section of hair that still clumped around it, the superglue still holding on. The man must have seen her puzzled expression; he tapped the side of his own head. 'The cut...'

'Oh... that. Fine.'

'Right, I'll be off then. That should do it.' He looked up at the ceiling, checking out his handiwork from within.

They stood in Ida's living room, neither of them used to conversation and both of them all too comfortable with the quiet. She noticed his hands were stuffed in his pockets and his eyes were skimming the room, taking in the place she'd called home for the past three years. She followed his gaze, suddenly embarrassed at the untidiness.

'It's a mess,' she said.

'It'll dry out.'

'What's your name?' Ida asked. She'd been wanting to know, feeling as though she needed to refer to him – if only in her own head – as something other than 'The Man', especially now that he'd temporarily fixed her roof.

He seemed to pause, thinking, and Ida wondered whether he'd simply forgotten his own name; living in such solitary conditions can make you forget a lot about yourself – your sense of humour, your interests, your fears. Maybe it could also make you forget your name.

'Walker.'

'Walker?'

He nodded, and Ida took it to mean that the conversation was over; he had given her a little part of himself – his surname, presumably – but that was all he was willing to divulge. Ida thought it was funny how he would happily walk miles to retrieve the tarp then spend his time fixing her roof when she had nothing to give him in return, yet his reluctance came in telling her his name. Ida understood: there was so little to protect nowadays, personal information became sacred, to be traded like secrets.

Walker didn't ask Ida for her name and she didn't offer it, she simply followed him outside as he left and went to move the generator, exposing the other side to the sun. When she'd finished, she saw the man was still standing there, watching.

'You got food?' he asked.

'I've got food,' she said, suddenly unsure whether he was expecting something; a payment of some sort.

'That you don't need to heat?' he asked, gesturing towards the generator.

Ida shrugged, thinking. She had some crackers and cereals and a few tins of fruit. She'd manage.

'Caught a rabbit this morning,' he said. 'I'll be eating around sunset – there'll be some spare, if you need it.'

'Oh,' Ida said, suddenly understanding. 'Right.' She tucked her hair behind her ears and watched as Walker turned to leave, picking his stick up as he did.

She looked up at the sky and towards the sun which now hung to the west – late afternoon, Ida thought. She sat down on the step and watched the man and the dog as they moved further and further away. She couldn't remember the last time she'd eaten meat – she had the occasional tin of corned beef or chilli, but she hadn't eaten fresh meat since before they came here.

After a while she stood and looked at the house and the sheet of blue now covering one side of the roof, ugly but reassuring. The ladder wasn't there anymore and Ida looked around the side of the house, noting that he'd put it back under the awning. She walked back inside and gathered the toolbox and hammer, returning them to their spot in the bathroom.

The air felt cold and damp, as though it was clinging to her skin as she padded through the house. She felt dingy; her robe smelled musty from the rain and her hair trailed over her shoulders, lank and greasy. She looked down at her feet and at the mud which still clung to them. She needed to wash but she had no way of heating the water and she didn't relish the thought of the cold temperatures of the river; the winds from the storm had penetrated her bones and left an icy trail.

She went into the bedroom and found a flannel in the cupboard, then she took one of the big bottles of water from the bathroom and slipped a half-used bar of soap into her pocket. She lugged the bottle outside using her uninjured arm and set it down at the back of the house. She looked at it – one of the big five-litre bottles she never had any use for before – knowing that Cal would tell her not to use her emergency supply for *washing*. She realised it wasn't an emergency, but she ached to feel clean and wash off the turmoil of the previous twenty-four hours. She would need to replace the water as soon as possible – she would boil some from the river as soon as she could use the generator and pour it into the bottle once it had cooled.

She wet the flannel and rubbed some soap into it until she'd worked up a lather. She started by washing her face then her neck and under her arms, moving down until she came to her feet. She poured water on them and scrubbed until they were clean. She checked around the house to make sure no one was there then she quickly dropped her robe and tipped her head upside down, pouring water through her hair. She stood completely naked as she had many times before, only now she felt exposed. Knowing that Walker was out there somewhere – just one person in the vast expanse of land – made her feel surprisingly less alone. She poured the rest of the water over her body, rinsing away the soap.

Shivering but clean, she went back into the house and closed all of the windows and doors. She took a pair of grey leggings and a beige half-zip jumper out of her wardrobe, dressed and climbed into bed, closing the curtains and shutting out the world. Sleep was calling her. As she drifted off she thought about Walker and his offer of a hot meal, her mouth watering at the thought of it. She decided, almost subconsciously, that she would let her body decide which she required more. If she woke before sunset, she would go, and if she didn't, she would enjoy the sweet relief of sleep.

CHAPTER SIXTEEN

W hen Ida woke it wasn't the gradual release from sleep that she'd grown accustomed to, it was sharp and sudden; one minute she was dreaming about an impending storm and the next her eyes were wide open, taking in the reality which she couldn't decide whether or not she preferred. She sat up and pulled back the curtain, looking out at the hills to the south. Darkness was descending, the skies dulling as the sun crept below the horizon, spilling crimson streaks among the high clouds. Her tummy growled as though remembering Walker's offer. She hadn't eaten all day and her energy levels had plummeted. She wanted to roll over and go back to sleep but the dull ache in her tummy told her it wouldn't come easily – she needed food.

She walked into the kitchen and looked aimlessly through one cupboard and then another, browsing the options she already knew were there. She could eat here – it wouldn't be the best meal she'd ever had but she could make do; a tin of fruit and some crackers or the five bean salad with some lettuce from the garden. She put her hand to her belly and felt the gentle rumblings. 'Okay, okay,' she conceded. She shut the cupboards, grabbed her coat and went outside. Her boots still hung on the line along with the other things she'd put out to dry. She gathered them all up and put them back inside before she left, not trusting the clouds which looked uncertain as they lingered above.

Her boots were still damp. She couldn't decide which would be better – bare feet or damp shoes. She opted for the latter, pulling them on over a pair of dry wool socks. She shut the front door and began walking north. The fields were undulating, a slight hill up to the dirt track which descended gradually on the other side, a gentle slope to Walker's. When she reached the crest, where the fields met the gravelly track which reminded her of Cal, she stopped for a moment, wondering what he would say if he knew what she was about to do. Cal's imaginary protestations filled her head and almost made her turn around, but the ache in her belly spurred her on. She reasoned that Walker couldn't be carrying the virus or she would have fallen ill by now – she'd had more than enough contact with him to have been exposed. He was a recluse, like her, so he didn't pose a risk in that way.

Ida reflected – not for the first time – on how her idea of risk had changed so dramatically. When she was in her early twenties, meeting her friends for a night out on the town, going back to a strange man's house in the middle of nowhere would have been unthinkable – especially someone like Walker. He didn't exactly look like the type of man parents would want their children dating or associating with. He was the sort of man who people gave a wide berth to. If Ida would have seen him on the streets of Surrey a few years ago, she would have thought he was homeless or recently released from prison, and now here she was voluntarily wandering into his house and eating his food. She reasoned that if he wanted to kill her, he would have done it before now. He'd had more than enough opportunity –

not least when she was unconscious on his couch or when he was in possession of a hammer earlier that day.

As she navigated the undulant fields, still damp and slippery from the rain, she noticed a streak of smoke in the distance coming from just behind Walker's hut. It was barely noticeable in the fading light, the view obstructed by the gathering of trees and shrubberies, but now that she was getting closer she could just make it out, and she could smell it too. She edged round the side of the hut, suddenly worried about what she might find.

Walker was sat back on a garden chair, the heels of his boots resting on a crate and a firepit just beside him. He turned as she rounded the corner but his expression remained unchanged and she suddenly felt as though she'd intruded.

'You came,' he said.

'I came. I can go if...'

Walker interrupted. 'Just surprised to see you is all.'

'I'm surprised to see *anyone*.'

She thought she saw the corners of his mouth turn into a smile, but it was fleeting. The firelight danced in his eyes as he stared straight ahead to the north, as though watching something in the distance. She followed his gaze but there was nothing to see; the land turned to rolling hills up ahead, obscuring where she knew the dirt track met with the road.

'It should be ready soon,' he said, gesturing towards the meat which sat atop of the firepit, skewered with what looked to be tomatoes and onions. Ida could smell it, the mild metallic scent mixed with the tang of the onions. It reminded her of being at a barbeque, the sun glaring down as she sat cross-legged on a deck chair, a cocktail glass held in her hand – it felt like another life rather than a distant memory.

'Smells good,' she said.

He leant down and picked up a glass bottle which clinked

against the chair leg as he lifted it. Ida watched as he took a long gulp – the greenish bottle, the red label...

'Is that *beer*?' she asked.

'You want one?' He didn't wait for an answer. On the other side of his chair was a bucket full of water with several bottles suspended in it. He took one out and undid the top on the side of the table, passing it to her.

She sat down on the empty chair beside him and took it. 'I haven't had one of these in years,' she said, sipping from the bottle. It tasted good – better than she remembered. It wouldn't have been her drink of choice typically, but now that she thought about it that wasn't because of the taste but rather due to the image. She always felt more ladylike with a glass of wine or a fancy cocktail. She wondered now why she ever cared; it seemed so trivial. So pointless.

'How's the roof?' Walker asked.

'Better without the hole in it.' She took another drink of her beer. 'Thanks,' she added. It was fast and quiet but there it was, the thank you she'd been wanting to say to him. She took a deep breath, realising she didn't feel as though she'd given any part of herself away by expressing her gratitude.

Walker nodded but didn't say anything. They sat like that for a while, the sky darkening until it revealed the stars. The clouds still loomed but they'd scattered, whispers of the storm remaining as though she needed a reminder. Ida took off her coat and sat back in the chair, the beer cradled in her hands. It was a warm evening, still and peaceful. She rested her head back, admiring the stars as she often did. When she glanced sideways at Walker she saw that he was doing the same, his head turned up towards the sky.

'What can you see?' she asked, then instantly regretted it. He wasn't Cal, nor was he her friend.

'Orion's Belt,' he answered, much to Ida's surprise. 'The hunter.'

'He's a hunter?' she asked.

'I don't know. Depends whether you believe Greek mythology I guess.'

'From what I remember, it's full of chaos and destruction. I'd say it sounds pretty accurate.'

Walker turned to face her and held out his bottle. 'To hiding from it all,' he said. She held out her bottle and tapped it against his, the clinking of the glass sharp against the stillness of the night. The wind had died down but the water still rushed, the river remembering the storm for much longer than the land.

Walker stood and placed his bottle down on the table, stepping over to the firepit and prodding at the skewers with a pair of metal tongs. Clearly deciding they were ready, he removed them from the fire and placed them on a large rectangular plate. Ida edged forward in her seat, her stomach so empty it hurt.

'Just got to let the skewers cool,' he said. 'You're hungry, huh?'

'I haven't eaten since...' she had to think about it for a moment, 'yesterday morning.' She'd had a handful of mixed nuts with her morning tea, sat doing a jigsaw in the blissful ignorance of what was about to come. It seemed such a long time ago now.

Walker tossed some wood onto the firepit and stoked it before sitting down and reaching into the bucket for another beer. Ida took another drink of hers and felt her shoulders loosen, the tension easing. 'You want another?' he asked.

'Don't you want to save them?' They were a precious commodity now, she didn't want to be taking something from him that he couldn't replace.

Walker looked puzzled and shook his head. 'Not

particularly.' He reached into the bucket and took out another, undoing the top before passing it to her.

Ida sat with a bottle of beer in each hand and a plateful of food in front of her, feeling like she'd hit the jackpot. She drained the first bottle and placed it on the table.

Walker leant forward and felt one of the skewers, apparently satisfied they wouldn't burn her. 'Tuck in,' he said, sliding the plate across to her.

Ida reached out and grabbed one. She couldn't help herself, she wanted to take it slow and relish the flavours, but she was too hungry. Walker took one for himself and leant back in his chair, taking his time, clearly not eating with the same urgency as Ida who chewed greedily, barely stopping to swallow. She finished the first and placed the empty skewer beside the plate, hoping Walker would encourage her to take another.

'Don't hold back on my account.' Walker wiped the grease from his mouth with the back of his hand and she noticed he'd barely made a dint in his.

She gulped down a mouthful of beer then took another from the plate. The onions were soft, the tomatoes sweet, and the meat was juicy and tender, cooked just the way she liked it. She couldn't remember the last time she'd enjoyed a meal this much.

'It's so good,' she said, her mouth full of the food and her head fuzzy from the beer.

'Glad you're enjoying it.' He placed his empty skewer down on the table and wiped his hands on his T-shirt.

'Aren't you going to have another?'

'I think you need it more than I do,' he said casually. Ida understood there was no deep and meaningful sentiment behind it but rather an observation; she was hungry, he was not so. He seemed to sense her apprehension. 'I've got plenty to eat if I'm hungry later. Go ahead.' He gestured to the plate where the last skewer remained, loaded with meat and vegetables.

Ida took it, enjoying the feeling of being full almost as much as the feeling of being less alone. She didn't need him to talk; she wasn't sure if she even wanted him to. She didn't need him to sit close or offer her things to eat or drink. It was enough to know that all this land wasn't as vacant as she'd believed, and this big wide world wasn't quite as cruel.

CHAPTER SEVENTEEN

After Ida had finished eating and drained her second beer, Walker got up and added some more wood to the fire then pulled another couple of bottles out of the bucket, leaving it empty.

'Another?' Walker asked.

Ida wanted another. She definitely wanted another. But the logical part of her mind – which was slightly less straight-thinking than usual but still functioning – told her it was a long walk home in the dark. She didn't fear the land, but she respected it, and she needed her wits about her for that. A fall in the night could leave her vulnerable, open to the elements and the weather she couldn't predict. Exposure could kill her out there, with no one to notice she was even gone.

'I'd better not,' she said reluctantly. 'Long walk back and it's already gone to my head.'

Walker put the bottle down on the table in front of her rather than back in the bucket. 'Got a torch?' he asked.

She pulled it out of her pocket and held it up to show him.

'Small torch for such a lot of land,' he said.

'Small doesn't necessarily mean weak.' She turned it on and pointed the beam of light away from the fire, out to the west where the darkness lurked, the river running somewhere beneath it. The nights were so absolute out in the midst of nothing, the absence of any light oppressive and suffocating. Cal had brought the torch with them when they came to the house; it was powerful and robust and it had come to her aid many times. She looked back over to Walker who raised his eyebrows.

'Not bad,' he conceded.

Ida felt a spot of rain fall on the top of her head. She looked up to the sky to see that clouds had blown over from the east, blocking the milky light of the moon and the stars which surrounded it.

'Rain,' Walker commented, more to himself than to Ida.

Before she'd had a chance to gather herself and think about the journey home, the spotting of rain had turned into a downpour. The firepit sizzled in protest and turned to smoke. Walker gathered his things off the table and opened the door to his place, Chief rushing inside. Walker looked back to Ida who sat there in the rain, wondering what on earth she should do. The alcohol had slowed her reactions and blurred her thinking. She knew she needed to get home fast; it would be a cold night on the fields if she lost her way.

'You coming?' he shouted over the noise of the rain.

Ida stood. 'I... I should go.' She looked around aimlessly, trying to think straight.

Before Walker could reply there was a crack of lightning over the forest; the sudden ferocity of it made Ida jump and cower away from it, moving over to Walker and the refuge of his hut. She thought about her house and the already fragile roof, the blue plastic sheet the only thing protecting it from flooding once more. She looked back to the forest and then to Walker who stood with the door held ajar, waiting for her to make up her mind.

She was soaked, her hair sticking to her forehead and her jumper clinging to her skin. She thought of the damage the lightning had done to her house and couldn't help but fear the damage it could do to her. As if encouraging her to make up her mind, the lightning came again, followed by a deep rumble of thunder. She took one last look over her shoulder, grabbed her coat off the chair, and went inside.

Walker let the door slam shut behind him. He walked to the other side of the room and set the plate and skewers down on top of the kitchen worktop, if you could call it a kitchen – it consisted of two cupboards with a makeshift board on top. Ida stood by the door dithering in her wet clothes, her arms folded across her chest, her coat clutched in her hand. Walker didn't seem to notice at first, he was too busy tending to the things he usually did alone. Ida suddenly realised there was a light on overhead, a single bulb casting an artificial glow around the small room.

'You have electricity?' she asked him. She hadn't expected him to. She looked around, searching for things he might want to power, beside the light – but she couldn't see anything. He had an open fire for heat and he obviously hunted for food which he cooked on the firepit – his one luxury must be light.

'Solar panels out back.' He gestured to the east. 'Just a couple.'

'What do you use it for?'

He stopped what he was doing and looked from Ida to the light above her and then back again.

'Just the light?' she asked.

'No, not just the light,' he replied, but he didn't elaborate. 'Here.' He'd been rummaging around in a large box, rifling through clothes she assumed were for himself, but instead he was holding a black T-shirt out to her. She reached out slowly, taking it from him and looking around the house to see where he expected her to change. 'I'm going to tidy up outside.' He opened the door and walked out into the night, Chief at his heels, his loyal follower.

Ida could hear him outside collecting the bottles, the sound of glass chinking against glass carrying through the walls. She held out the T-shirt in front of her – completely unremarkable, plain black and oversized even for Walker. She held it close to her face and smelled it, expecting something entirely different to the fresh scent she found there. It was clean and dry and that was enough for Ida. She pulled her jumper over her head and then her sports bra, dropping them to the floor beside her and pulling on the T-shirt. She checked the length of it against her legs – it came almost to her knees. She debated for a moment, kicking off her boots as her hands felt her wet leggings, then she pulled them off too.

Walker appeared back in the room just as she'd tossed them all into one big pile. He was wet through, his face red and his clothes dripping rain onto the floor. There was another crack of lightning outside which seemed to be coming from the forest, the storm still lingering nearby.

'There are blankets on the bed,' he said. Then without warning he pulled off his T-shirt, dropping it to the floor and rummaging around in the box. He took out an almost identical one and pulled it over his head without drying himself. Damp patches soaked into the material but he didn't seem to notice. He held up a dry pair of shorts and turned to Ida. 'You might want to...' He made a turning motion with his finger in the air in front of him.

'Oh, sorry, of course.' She turned round and faced the back wall – the kitchen area and the chair where she'd first seen Walker sitting. There was another strike of lightning followed almost immediately by a loud rumble of thunder.

'Done,' Walker shouted over it.

Ida turned round, rubbing at her bare arms, still cold from the rain.

'I'll get a fire going. You can dry your clothes.'

Ida sat down on the bed and draped a blanket around her – the one she remembered from all those weeks ago, navy-blue tartan with a fringe on either end. She watched Walker make a fire, slow but methodical – a job he'd done many times before. The warmth of it soon filled the room. He put a couple of crates in front of it and looked over to the pile of Ida's wet clothes but, seeing her bra lying on top, he clearly thought better of it.

'I'll let you...' he said, gesturing over to them.

Ida set the clothes out as best she could while Walker pulled the chair over from the back of the room, placing it down next to the bed. Ida suddenly felt like a burden, intruding on this man and his space, forcing him to sit on his chair rather than lie in his bed. Chief made his way over and lay in the orange glow of the fire beside Walker's feet. For the first time, Ida held out her hand and stroked his head. She'd been avoiding any contact without necessarily realising it but she couldn't put her finger on why. Maybe she was protecting herself – she loved dogs and didn't want to end up pining for one of her own. Or maybe, she thought, she just didn't want another reason to feel drawn to this place; to the hut and the food and the company.

'I'll leave once the storm's passed,' Ida said.

'Probably here for the night. Take the bed, I'm not tired.'

'I can't do that.'

'Sure you can.'

'But... where will you sleep?'

'I'm not tired.'

'But... you will be at some point.'

'Then I can sleep on the floor.' He saw that Ida was about to protest and added: 'I've slept in worse places.'

Ida sighed and sat on the bed, stuck between the fatigue that had crept in slowly at first and then all of a sudden – spurred on by the warmth of the fire and the two bottles of beer – and the uncomfortable feeling in her chest which told her she shouldn't be here. Her shoulder ached. She pulled the T-shirt to the side and saw that the bruise had darkened; it looked angry against her porcelain skin. She wrapped the blanket around her shoulders and rested her back against the wall. She hadn't quite decided whether to sleep or not, but she thought she might as well get comfy while she made up her mind.

'How long have you been living here?' Ida asked, not sure whether she expected him to answer.

Walker was slouched back in his chair, his long legs stretched out in front of him, one ankle crossed over the other. Ida noticed he was wearing a pair of thick wool socks with several holes in them. He seemed to be thinking about how long he'd been living here, his skin tinged orange by the glow of the fire. Ida understood Walker's uncertainty; in those long weeks between Cal's visits she could easily lose track of time, only stopping to notice the passing of the days to try and predict when he'd be back.

'Years,' he said finally. Ida waited to see whether he was going to try and narrow it down any further, but he didn't.

The warmth seeped out into the room, filling all the empty spaces and making Ida's eyes feel heavy and dry. The thunder carried on rumbling but the sound was drifting further and further away. It was passing, but the rain was not, it lashed heavily against the roof and the window, filling the room with a harsh drumming sound. Chief slept peacefully, his chest rising and falling as Walker watched the flames dance in the fireplace.

Ida's mind drifted briefly to her house and the makeshift roof; she hoped it had withstood the storm. She hoped she would return to dry floors and a generator that had avoided the onslaught of rain. She tried to remember how she'd positioned it – under the awning and close to the stone wall. She hoped it was safe.

And as she drifted off to sleep, she hoped she was, too.

CHAPTER EIGHTEEN

Ida woke to an empty room. At some point during the night she'd lain down on the bed, the blanket pulled up over her. She stretched, feeling the warmth of the sheets against her bare legs. The fire was out and daylight was flooding in through the window; the sheet which hung there was now hooked back onto a nail in the wall. She looked outside but she couldn't see Walker, just the sprawling fields and the rising sun to the east.

There was a table beneath the window, old and wooden, and on top of it lay a couple of books. Ida examined them, relishing the thought of new things to read then admonishing herself for assuming she would borrow them – that they would have the kind of neighbourly relationship which facilitated such things. This wasn't a world where people swapped books or shared recipes, it was a world where food was scarce and humanity and goodwill were even scarcer.

She tried to remember something Cal had said to her three years before, when they'd been deciding whether to stay and hunker down or get out before it was too late. Ida had wanted to stay, to show some solidarity with the community they'd become part of. *Do you really want to be here when the food and water and the medication run out? That's when people show their true colours, Ida, when it's do or die.*

She heard clattering outside the door and the low rumbling of Walker's voice drifting through it. She edged closer, listening.

'Good boy, Chief,' she could hear him saying. 'It'll be ready soon.' She opened the door to find Walker stood at the firepit. He didn't turn to look at her but rather carried on poking and prodding whatever was cooking. 'Morning,' he said.

'Morning.' It was bright but cool, the sun low in the sky – it was still early. The aroma of what Walker was heating on the fire drifted over to greet her. 'Smells good,' she said.

'Caught a squirrel this morning but it's for Chief I'm afraid.'

Ida grimaced – she hadn't realised squirrel meat could smell so good. Walker took it off the firepit and scraped it into a bowl. 'Got to cool yet, boy,' he told Chief who was sat waiting eagerly beside him. 'Sleep well?' he asked, turning to Ida.

'I think so, what about you? Did you get any sleep?'

'Sure.' He sat down on one of the chairs they'd used the night before. 'I'm going to heat some porridge soon,' he said. 'You're welcome to have some.'

'Oh no, I couldn't, I've already intruded enough.'

'Intruded implies you were uninvited.' Walker looked at her. 'I invited you,' he clarified.

'Well, if you're sure... if you have enough...'

'I have plenty.' And with that he got up and went inside. Ida followed him in and took the clothes off the crate, feeling the material. 'Dry?' he asked.

Ida nodded. Walker took a bag of oats out of his cupboard along with a pan, a bottle of water and a little glass jar containing an amber liquid. 'Is that *honey*?' she asked.

'Yeah, I can make yours without if you prefer?'

'No, I love honey, I just haven't had it in ages.'

Walker either didn't notice her giddiness or chose to ignore it. 'I'll be outside.'

Ida changed quickly then folded the T-shirt she'd borrowed and placed it on the bed, tidying the blankets and the pillows and putting the chair back in the corner. When she'd finished she went outside to find Chief tucking into his meal and Walker stirring a pot on the firepit. Ida sat on one of the chairs and breathed in the fresh scent left by the thunder. The birds were loud this morning and the river rough and wild, nature re-emerging after the storm, stronger than ever.

Neither of them spoke until the food was ready, choosing to listen to the world rather than each other. Walker ladled thick porridge into a bowl and passed it to Ida, eating his own portion straight from the pot.

'Have I used your only bowl?' she asked.

'Bowl, pan... all the same to me.' Ida took that to mean *yes.*

It was amazing the difference a good dollop of honey could make to the oats; Ida had spent so long eating it plain or with a few blackberries or strawberries tossed in that it almost tasted too sweet. Almost.

'You don't have much good food at your place, huh?' Walker spoke with his mouth full, bits of white porridge clinging to the thick hairs on his chin.

'Not really. Tins, mostly.'

Walker nodded as though he understood, but she wasn't sure that he did. Maybe she should learn to hunt. Ida scraped her bowl clean then put it down on the table. 'Thank you for breakfast, and for dinner last night. And the shelter.'

The list could have been so much longer, Ida realised, but she cut it short, not wanting to embarrass either of them; Walker didn't strike her as someone who needed or wanted a lot of recognition.

'No bother,' he said. Chief wandered over and sat between

them, his eyes on the pan of porridge; Walker took a spoonful and let it drop onto the floor. 'There you go, bud.'

Ida couldn't help but smile.

'You always had Chief out here with you?'

'Yep. Always.'

Ida wanted to ask him how old Chief was but she realised she was just being nosy, trying to pry into how long Walker had lived here – she wasn't sure why she wanted to know, it just felt like information she should be armed with. Did she come to his land or he hers? She realised that in reality it was neither; there were miles between them, the kind of distance that would have seemed unimaginable back in Surrey.

'Think I'm going to go for a swim,' Walker said suddenly, putting the empty pan down on the table.

'You swim in there?' She gestured over towards the river; she could hear it rushing and swelling at the banks.

'You don't?' He seemed surprised.

Ida shook her head. 'It's not really deep enough by the house.'

'It's deep enough here.'

He got up and walked towards the river, leaving Ida sat wondering whether she should follow. Chief didn't hesitate, he was soon at Walker's heels as he strode barefoot across the grass. It wasn't far; the hut sat between the dirt track over to the south-east and the river to the west, a mere two hundred metres or so away. Ida's curiosity got the better of her and she got up and followed him.

She reached him as he was undressing, pulling off his T-shirt right there at the water's edge. Ida looked away, unsure what to do, choosing instead to look out over the flow of the river and the forest beyond.

'You coming?' Walker didn't wait for a reply, he kicked off

his trousers to reveal a pair of boxer shorts then jumped in without looking back.

It seemed to take him a while to resurface. Ida's eyes darted around looking for him, then seconds later his head appeared above the water.

'Cold?' Ida asked.

'Not so bad.' He swam with the current, further south towards her house, then when the depth began to taper away he turned and swam back towards her.

Chief looked at her questioningly, his ears pricked. 'Oh what the hell,' Ida muttered. She pulled off her jumper and let it fall to the ground revealing her old sports bra, then she kicked off her leggings and stood at the water's edge in her pants, her toes curling as she tried to pluck up the courage to jump in. It was totally out of character for Ida – crazy and wild and all of the things she saw in the land around her but which she suppressed in herself. She should have felt exposed stood half naked like that. She should have felt foolish and vulnerable and irrational. But she didn't – she felt free.

Walker swam towards her, his head bobbing in and out of the river. When he reached her, he stopped and began treading water, but he didn't say anything. Ida dipped her foot in the water and moved it back and forth, getting used to the temperature. She ran her fingers through her hair and took a deep breath, her eyes fixed on a space in front of her. She was thinking about what was underneath – the unknown – not the cold which she knew would greet her. In that moment of apprehension, she'd allowed her mind to wander. It was always the way with Ida, her anxieties clutching onto the things she didn't know and often couldn't control, forcing her to walk away rather than find out. She should have gone with the initial thrill of it all rather than let the decision linger.

'Just got to keep moving,' Walker shouted. 'That's all.'

'Right,' whispered Ida. 'Keep moving.' Then she jumped.

The water wasn't as cold as she'd been expecting, but it was still cold enough to catch her breath. She plummeted through the water until her feet grazed the gravelly bottom of the riverbed, then she kicked against it and soared to the surface, gasping for breath and pushing her hair from her face. She kicked her legs to keep herself afloat and when she opened her eyes she saw Walker doing the same, just across from her. The water had tamed his hair the way it had Ida's, limp strands stuck to his forehead and face; but that wasn't the only reason he looked different – he was smiling. It changed his face – the shape and his eyes which lit up with it.

'What?' Ida asked.

Walker didn't respond, he just shrugged and swam north against the current. Ida followed, the water splashing in her face and the occasional twig or reed skimming her legs. They swam past Walker's hut until the river began to arc and she noticed Walker suddenly stopped swimming, now able to touch the floor again. Ida swam past him until she felt her own feet could touch the floor, then she turned to face him.

'You've got to keep moving,' he said, then he dived under the water and swam back the way they'd come. Ida's heart was thudding and her breathing was fast and shallow, but she felt alive with endorphins. She realised that – stood in her pants and bra, swimming with a stranger in the river that had sustained her – she was smiling. She threw herself forward into the sanctuary of the water and began to swim, this time with the current there to help guide her.

CHAPTER NINETEEN

They ran back towards Walker's hut with their clothes clutched to their chests, their bare feet pounding against the grass. Ida was freezing and her whole body shook with it, unable to be stilled. Chief raced along beside them, his tail wagging.

Once they got inside Walker threw her a towel as big as a blanket; she wrapped it around herself and sat down on one of the crates, not wanting to dampen the bed. When she turned back round, Walker was dressed in a hoody and a pair of shorts and she realised she'd probably taken his only towel. He didn't say anything, so neither did she.

'I'll make us a warm drink,' he said, disappearing outside.

Ida sat shivering for a while before she plucked up the courage to take off her wet underwear and get dressed. She found her coat from the night before on the floor and put that on, too, the outer layer still a little damp from the rain. Outside the hut, the firepit was gently heating a pan of water while Walker threw a stick for Chief. Ida watched him give chase, running out to the north, towards the road which Ida knew ran beyond the hills. She could see the joy Walker got from Chief and the bond they shared; Ida couldn't help but feel envious. Having someone depend on you, someone to get up for in a morning – she thought it must be nice to have a purpose other than survival.

'Hope you like it black,' Walker said.

'Coffee?' she asked.

'Yep.'

'Please tell me you have two mugs?'

Walker smiled. 'Actually it's one of the few things I doubled up on.' He handed her a blue-and-white-striped mug and they both sat down on the chairs outside, enjoying the warmth that had begun to gather in the sun.

'You swim a lot?' Ida asked him.

'Sure I do,' he said. 'Not many people have a river in their back garden.'

'No, I don't suppose they do. I'm surprised I've never seen you before; I've got a pretty good view of the river from my place.'

'I've seen *you* before,' he said simply.

'You have?' She cradled the mug, letting the heat gather in her hands.

'Yep. Saw you and...' he seemed to search for the right word, 'your man friend... arrive here. Saw him coming and going.'

Ida couldn't help but laugh. 'My man friend?'

Walker shrugged. 'Well, whatever he is.'

'My fiancé,' she said. She realised how alien that word sounded now, she hadn't used it in so long. 'He's in the military so he comes whenever he can get leave.'

Walker nodded but didn't ask any more questions. Ida wasn't surprised, he still didn't know her name and didn't seem interested in finding out.

'I saw your books...' she said.

'Oh yeah?'

'I have some up at the house, but they got a little wet in the flood.' She wasn't sure if she was asking to borrow one of his or whether she was just testing the water.

'Take any from the piles on the floor,' he said simply. 'The ones on the table I'm part way through.'

'You read a lot?' she asked.

'Yep.'

'Got to fill your time out here.'

'A good book will do that.'

'I couldn't help noticing you don't have a lot of... things.'

Walker took a long drink from his mug. 'It's one of the great deceptions of our time, don't you think?'

'What is?'

'That we need so much to live.'

Ida thought about it for a moment, trying to recall her house in Surrey, so full of the things she believed she needed. She tried to remember what it was like.

'There's nothing you miss?' she asked.

Walker shrugged, staring out across the fields. She took that as his response – a simple shrug accounting for the things he recalled but had decided he didn't need – but then he spoke. 'Ice for my whisky.'

Ida laughed. 'Not the answer I was expecting.'

'What about you?' he asked.

She thought about it for a moment though she already knew the things she craved the most. 'A hot bath. Chocolate cake. And a cold can of Coke.' She left off the long list of people. 'Oh, and music,' she added.

Walker smiled. 'Now one of those I can help with.'

Ida raised her eyebrows questioningly but Walker didn't respond, he simply got up and strode into the house. Ida sat waiting, an excitement she tried to quash simmering in her belly. She finished her drink and put the mug on the table.

There were a few minutes of quiet except for the birdsong and the flow of the river, the occasional whistle of the wind blowing through the trees. Then quite suddenly, it was drowned out by the sound of music. Walker reappeared in the doorway, his shoulder resting against the wooden frame. Fleetwood Mac blasted out and Ida's mouth fell open.

'I save the electricity for the record player,' he said.

'I knew there must be something!'

Ida stood, walking back and forth along the grass, suddenly unable to keep still.

'Beer?' Walker asked, but he didn't wait for a response. He disappeared round the side of the hut and, her curiosity piqued, Ida followed. There was a shed built onto the side, fairly big and windowless. On top were a couple of solar panels. Walker disappeared inside and returned with two beers. 'They're warm,' he said. 'But I've got used to warm beer.'

'No ice?' she asked, smirking.

Walker smiled and carried the bottles round to the front, opening them on the table and passing one to Ida. They sat down just as one song ended and another began.

'"Dreams",' Ida said. She listened to Stevie Nicks's smooth voice singing about the sound of loneliness. 'This song reminds me of...' Her voice trailed away, memories she didn't want to acknowledge pushing to the surface. 'Never mind,' she said, taking a drink from the bottle.

She'd thought of her friend Ellen whose dad had been a huge Fleetwood Mac fan. The song reminded her of being at their house and hearing it playing loudly in the lounge, Ellen's mum shouting at him from the kitchen to turn it down while Ida and Ellen sat looking at magazines. Listening to their music now, Ida felt the sweet stirrings of nostalgia – for her friend; for her childhood; for life before. The familiar churnings always started off quite pleasant but Ida knew by now that they soon spiralled into hopeless longing.

'One of the best bands of all time,' Walker said, and Ida was grateful to him for not asking exactly what the song had reminded her of. They didn't need to say anything else, they were just happy to enjoy the music. It was as though they'd travelled back in time; two old friends enjoying a beer outside of a bar. It wasn't the presence of company that Ida was enjoying as much as the absence of being alone. She realised she'd become so numb to it that she hadn't recognised how much it was weighing her down.

They sat and listened to the whole album, then when their bottles were empty and the sounds of nature had returned, Ida stood. 'I should get going,' she said, though she made no attempt to move.

'Sure,' Walker said. 'Don't forget the books.'

'Only if you're sure it's okay.'

'Help yourself.'

Ida wandered back inside and scanned the spines of the books that were all piled on top of each other haphazardly in four towering piles. 'Any recommendations?'

He knelt down beside her and pulled a few out, none of which she'd heard of before. He handed them to her and she stood, grabbing her damp underwear which she'd left on top of the towel by the fireplace.

'Right. Well, thank you.'

'No bother,' Walker said. He'd let the door close shut behind him and, noticing Ida's hands were full, he opened it for her.

'I'll return these once I've read them,' she said.

'You don't have to.'

Ida wasn't sure whether he was insinuating that he didn't want her to return the books because he didn't want her to return to the hut at all, but something told her that wasn't the case and that he was just being kind, putting no pressure on her to do anything she didn't want to. She walked outside past the chairs and the table before turning back to him. 'Bye,' she said simply.

He held up his hand briefly then disappeared inside, the door banging shut behind him.

Ida carried her things, new and old, back to her house, wondering what she might find when she got there. She was pleasantly surprised; it was the best she could have hoped for, all four walls still standing and the tarp still held in place. When she opened the door she was greeted by the smell of damp but the floors appeared dry at least. She set the books down on top of the wood mantel then returned outside to hang her underwear out to dry.

She checked on the generator which seemed dry to the touch but Ida knew she wouldn't be able to trust it for at least another couple of days; she couldn't be sure how wet it had got during the second storm and it wasn't worth the risk.

The vegetable patch looked well, the soil still damp from the rain. She bent down and plucked a lettuce leaf out of the ground, putting it straight into her mouth. It wasn't the meat and vegetable skewers or the porridge with honey, but it would have to do.

She spent the rest of the day pottering about the house. She dragged the sofa cushions back outside to finish drying in the sun then pegged the patchwork blanket out on the line. She cleaned down the worktops and the table and stacked her old books on the mantelpiece, their edges curled and browned, a stark contrast to the neat edges of Walker's which sat beside them. She changed and washed the clothes she'd had on using the water from the river, then she settled down on the sofa with one of her new books.

She hadn't heard of it before, it was called *The Quiet Space Between Us*. On the front was a woman with blonde hair walking away from an outstretched hand. There was a woodland in the distance, dark and menacing, the night surrounding them. Ida ran her fingers over the cover and the raised letters, taking it all in, then she read the blurb and the inside sleeve about the author. She always did this with new things – took her time. It wasn't until she was reading the small print that her heart seemed to skip a beat, her breath catching in her chest, the world momentarily suspended.

CHAPTER TWENTY

She ran back to Walker's place, stopping halfway to catch her breath. She clutched the book in her hands and opened the front page, checking, doubting herself the way she often did. She looked at the small print again, hoping that she'd somehow read it wrong, but she hadn't. It was still there in black and white, as obvious as it was confusing.

She closed it, gripping it tightly in one hand while she ran across the fields, past the dirt track and towards the river. She could hear music and see a thin trail of smoke coming from the other side of the hut but she couldn't see Walker. She ran round to the other side and found him there by the shed chopping wood. He was damp with sweat and his hair was tied back off his face. He looked at Ida, and Ida looked at him.

'Where did you get this?' she demanded, holding the book up for him to see.

Walker's eyes narrowed, confused. 'What do you mean?'

'This book... where did you get it?' Ida was shouting over the sound of the music, the same record as earlier now playing a different song: 'Go Your Own Way'.

'A shop,' he said simply, the axe still held in his hand.

'But which shop... *when?*'

Walker scratched the back of his head and shrugged. 'The supermarket in town,' he said, gesturing over towards the hills and whatever lay beyond. 'I don't know when.'

'You don't know?'

'Why does it matter?'

She opened the front cover and thrust it at him. He leant the axe on a log and took it from her.

'The date,' she said. 'It was published this year!'

He looked from Ida to the book and then back. 'So?'

'So how is that possible?'

Walker looked genuinely confused which only frustrated Ida further. She wanted answers but they weren't coming as quickly and as clearly as she would like.

'I must have got it when I last went into town then,' he said simply. 'End of January, I think.'

'January *this* year?'

'Yes. January this year.' He spoke slowly, his voice low and devoid of all the anger that was so clear in Ida's.

'No. No. You're lying.'

'What... why would I lie about that?'

'How is that possible? How!' She was shouting at him, loud and angry. There was so much frustration and confusion bubbling away inside her that she had to release it somehow or she felt she would explode. 'How is it possible?' she repeated.

He put the book down on a log and took a step towards her. 'Are you okay?'

Ida could hear the concern in his voice and the calmness in his tone, as though he was scared he would break her if he spoke too loudly. She tried to think straight, to arrange her thoughts in some logical order that allowed her to ask the questions she needed, but she couldn't. She was spiralling, overloaded with information that didn't make sense.

'Do you need me to get you some help?' Walker asked her.

'Help? What do you mean?'

'The guy... your fiancé... he mentioned you have some...' he paused, trying to find the right words, trying not to aggravate her further, 'some health issues.'

'What? No. No. *I'm* not the one with health issues.'

Walker's eyes narrowed again. Ida paced around the grass, walking backwards and forwards, trying to allay some of the tension and the stress. She ran both hands through her hair, her fingertips applying pressure to her head which was beginning to throb.

'I don't understand,' Ida whispered, more to herself than to Walker.

'He told me that's why you live out here alone.'

Ida stopped walking and looked at him, her eyes wide and wild, searching for the truth she wasn't sure she would find out here. 'I'm...' she said, then took a deep breath. 'I'm here to keep safe, to avoid catching the virus.'

'What virus?' Walker's brow furrowed. 'You mean the flu strain a few years back? Is that why you're here?'

Ida nodded almost imperceptibly.

'You don't need to worry about that anymore, it's included in the yearly flu vaccines and there are treatments now. Medicines.'

'But I saw... it was chaos.'

'Yep. A rough year from what I heard.'

Ida shook her head. She couldn't believe what Walker was telling her because to believe him meant something so immeasurably cruel that she didn't know how she would ever recover from it. 'No,' she said blankly. 'No, you're lying. You're lying, you have to be lying!' Emotion raged in her voice, unable to be contained.

Walker strode past her, towards the front door. Ida waited, not knowing or caring whether he would return.

'Here,' he said, holding something out for her to take. Her vision was blurred by the tears which gathered there; she blinked them away, letting them fall freely down her cheeks. It was a newspaper, dated earlier that year – January twentieth. 'It's just the local one; I never usually buy them but there'd been an accident on the road and a helicopter had had to come and airlift someone to hospital.' He looked down at the ground, remembering. 'I stayed with them till the paramedics arrived – a young woman. I wanted to know what happened to her.'

Ida looked at the front page and an image of a crash on a winding country road. Then she remembered seeing a helicopter land earlier in the year; she'd told Cal about it. He'd told her it was military. She held the paper out in her trembling hands, flicking through the pages, looking for some mention of the world Cal had described. But there was nothing.

Ida's knees began to buckle. She felt faint and dizzy. Walker noticed her swaying and stepped towards her, supporting her weight. He helped her over to the chairs at the front of his hut and sat her down, then he disappeared inside. Chief remained next to Ida and she rested her hand on his head.

The newspaper lay on the table, blowing gently in the breeze. She stared at it, at what it represented, and then her eyes filled with tears once more. Walker returned with a glass of water and handed it to her. She sipped at it, trying to decide what to ask or what she should do. Should she leave? Should she stay? She couldn't decide, so instead she sat there with Walker and Chief, listening to the music and looking out to the hills. A long time passed before anyone spoke.

'Why would...?' Ida began, but her voice caught in her throat, a cry threatening to drown it out. She swallowed hard.

Walker knew the essence of her question. Why would

someone do this to her? Why would someone she loved keep her out here, feeding her with information that kept her a prisoner?

'He told me you're out here because you had a breakdown.'

Ida was numb. The information found her but she didn't react. She tried to let it settle, to seep into her mind, but it was as though she'd met her limit. She was at maximum capacity, unable to process anything further.

Ida took a big gulp of water then placed the glass on the table, standing up and walking towards the river.

'Where are you going?' Walker shouted after her.

'For a swim.'

She needed to feel something other than foolish, if only for a fleeting moment in time.

***

She hit the water with more force than last time, her jump fuelled by the anger and the lies. She let herself fall to the bottom and held her breath there for as long as she could. When she resurfaced, Walker was stood at the edge with a towel.

'I'll leave this here for you,' he said, then he turned and walked back to his place. Ida was grateful that he didn't stay, she needed to be alone, to feel the water whipping at her skin and hear the current rushing in her ears. She took a big gulp of air and dipped under the surface again.

A couple of years ago there'd been a lot of rain in November and the river had burst its banks further north, flooding the fields and carrying water past her house much faster than usual. Among the current she'd found bits of rubbish – a faded crisp packet and a plastic bottle, a ripped packet of sweets and a red-and-white-striped straw. She'd gathered up the litter to put in the bin she kept by the wood store; Cal would take it with him the next time he came.

When she picked the plastic bottle up she realised there was something inside it – a ticket, one of the square ones she used to get from the machine at a car park. The writing was faded and smeared, the paper damp, but still she tried to make it out, curious where this old relic of a past life had originated. She held it close to her face and looked at where the date was printed in the top left corner – it looked as though it was from the week before, purchased at a place Ida had never heard of. Ida had screwed up her face, her brow furrowing as she struggled to read it, certain that the smudged ink was skewing the date. Eventually, she hadn't trusted her eyes, shoving it into the bin along with the rest of the rubbish and never thinking any more of it.

She thought about it now, though, as her skin prickled from the coolness of the water and her hair floated in front of her face. She rose back above the surface and gulped greedily for air. Why hadn't she asked Cal about it a couple of years earlier when she'd found it? She'd trusted him so completely that she'd been blind to any evidence to the contrary.

She dived back underwater and screamed into the flow of the river, her tears invisible and her silent cries heard by no one. The water filled her ears and calmed her, holding her weight in a way no one could, suspending her in a moment of safety that Cal's lies couldn't reach. Her heart ached and her mind raced, but for one small moment she let it all go, surrendering herself to the river and allowing herself to feel nothing but its grip.

CHAPTER TWENTY-ONE

Ida sat beside the river with the towel draped over her shoulders, shivering. She was staring at a leaf that was caught against some shrubbery on the bank, watching as it was pushed and pulled by the current but seemed unable to break free. After a while, Walker joined her, passing her a steaming hot mug of black coffee but not saying anything, just sitting down beside her on the grassy bank. When she took a sip, she could taste the smooth sweetness of honey.

'I don't know what to do,' Ida whispered into the wind.

Walker took a deep breath and Ida felt a sudden pang of guilt for putting him in the difficult situation of trying to find the right words to comfort a stranger. Knowing what she now knew, she couldn't help but see Walker in a different light. He hadn't moved here out of necessity, he'd moved here through choice, presumably to avoid people – to live a simple, peaceful life. Or maybe he was running away from something of a different kind. Either way, Ida felt sure this hadn't been part of his plan.

'It's okay,' Ida said. 'I don't expect you to know the answer.' She finished her coffee then stood and wrapped the towel around her; it was so long it grazed against the grass. 'I should go.' She bent down and scooped up the clothes she'd left there.

Walker stood up and turned to look out towards the hills, then he turned back to face Ida. 'I might not be able to provide you with answers, but I have an idea.' He took the empty mug from Ida. 'Fancy a walk?'

It was not what she'd been expecting, though she didn't really know what to expect anymore. 'Sure.'

After heading back inside to dress, Ida went and waited for Walker outside. He emerged in a grey zip-up jacket with a backpack slung over his shoulder. 'See you later, Chief,' he shouted inside, locking the door behind him. 'Right, this way.'

They walked north-east, skimming the dirt track and coming to the foot of a hill. 'Quicker to go over,' Walker said. 'Otherwise it's another couple of miles east.'

They walked the steep incline, the coarse grass brushing at her ankles. About halfway up, it petered out, rolling into a steady climb over the peak. When they got to the top Ida stood and looked at the view. There was a narrow road below winding through the hills on either side. She could just make out some buildings in the distance, but the view was obscured by the land and the trees.

'Hamilton,' Walker said, following Ida's gaze. 'Nearest town, few miles further north.'

'Is that where we're going?' she asked. She felt nervous all of a sudden, her anxieties kicking in, making her want to turn around and run. She looked back over her shoulder, towards Walker's place and, further south, her own house, the only home she'd known for three long years.

'If you want to.'

'I don't know.'

'That's okay,' Walker said.

'Tell me about it. What's it like?' She wanted to visualise it, to set it out in her mind. To edge away at the unknown.

'It's more like a village really. Mostly residential. Supermarket, chemist, post office. Not a lot to most, but a little too much for me.'

Ida understood. It felt like a lot to her too.

'My truck's parked down there.' Walker pointed to a small square of land just off of the narrow road. It wasn't a car park as such, but it was more than a lay-by. 'We can go for a drive, see what you think?'

'Okay,' she said, but she didn't move and neither did Walker; he was waiting for her to be sure, to put one foot in front of the other. *You've got to keep moving.* His words came to her as she stood in indecision, a fire inside her that swelled in her chest. 'Okay,' she repeated, and this time she put one foot in front of the other and led the way.

Walker's truck was old and battered, a black Ford Ranger with a silver trim around the bottom. The seats were torn in places and the interior dusty; when Walker turned the ignition it grumbled and spluttered before the engine sprung to life. Before he released the handbrake, he turned to look at her.

'You sure?'

Ida nodded. She wasn't sure, exactly, but there was something inside her telling her she needed the truth to be sprawled out in front of her, stark and real. She didn't trust herself to believe more of Cal's lies if she hadn't convinced herself with irrefutable evidence first. Walker put the car in gear and eased out onto the road.

It felt strange at first, being back in a car, the smooth vibrations and the landscape racing by. Walker drove slowly, easing into the corners and taking his time. On more than one occasion Ida caught him glancing over at her – checking on her, she guessed.

'What happened to the woman?' Ida asked, remembering the crash on this road and what Walker had told her.

Walker took a deep breath before responding. 'She died.'

'Oh... I... I'm so sorry.'

Walker didn't respond, but Ida was sure she saw his eyes flicker, a glassiness to them that wasn't there before. She didn't press him further. They drove over a low bridge across the river, farmland stretching out on either side separated by drystone walls. Ida watched the young lambs skipping around the fields, their mothers grazing.

They passed a church on the right which stood back from the road, large and imposing, a cemetery wrapped around it and a sign at the front inviting people to attend the Sunday service. Ida had believed in God once, a long time ago, before her mother died and the world seemed suddenly harsh and cruel. Her lack of faith wasn't sudden, it didn't just disappear overnight, it lingered on for a while before fading to nothing. Ida watched the church as they passed, a failed protector, just like Cal.

All at once the scenery turned to residential, stone cottages sat right at the edge of the narrow road, hanging baskets and neat little name plaques adorning the fronts. Two elderly men stood outside one of them with a ladder leaning against the wall, looking up at something on the roof. Walker had to slow down to a crawl and edge around them; the men held their hands up to him and Ida wondered if they knew each other. As they eased out of the residential streets Ida saw a pub sat on a corner with white painted walls and a thatched roof, little wooden benches scattered around it. She watched as a couple disappeared inside through the arched doorway, hand in hand.

The supermarket seemed to be just outside of town at the

top of a hill. They parked at the front in the little car park, Ida in her own world of worry and Walker trying to break her free. It was a small place and not one that Ida recognised; a faded purple sign above the door and a single fuel pump at the far side. There was a poster in the window telling people to shop local and a sign lit up on the door declaring it open. Across the road stood a row of three shops, all small and narrow with old signs above the door. It was like a place that time forgot. Maybe it had. There were a few people coming and going and Ida felt herself panic, reacting to a threat they no longer posed. She breathed deeply, trying to overcome the fear, her hands clasped in her lap as she picked at her fingernails.

'Not all that far from Snowdon,' Walker said, following Ida's gaze to the shops across the road. 'Get a lot of tourist trade.'

Ida realised what he was referring to: one of the shops was called The Hiker's Hut, it had mannequins in the window modelling different walking gear and a selection of boots on a rack outside. She didn't respond; a memory had forced its way into her mind and taken over her thoughts, stinging at her chest and forcing her to relive something she thought she'd buried deep enough never to have to think about again.

It was a warm September day and the stillness of the ground had deceived Ida and Cal as they'd set off for the top of Snowdon. They'd thought they were prepared; they'd already climbed Scafell Pike and would be doing Ben Nevis last – the Three Peaks. At the top, snow clashed with the fog so they couldn't tell where one ended and the other began. It had caught them out and the descent had been perilous, fraught with frayed tempers and several near-misses and dangerous missteps. Ida was consumed by relief when they got back to the bottom, as though they'd narrowly escaped death. Maybe they had. Cal hadn't felt the same rush of euphoria. He was short-tempered with her as though it was her fault. In the car park Ida had seen a man loading his things into a car. She took out her phone and asked him to take a photo of them together. Cal had stood next to her, his jaw set, his body stiff and unwelcoming. She slipped her arm around his waist and felt him recoil at her touch.

The man had been friendly and chatty and all of the things that Cal, in that moment, wasn't. They'd talked about the climb and the conditions at the top and, all the while, Ida had been distracted by a heavy knot in her stomach. She was conscious of Cal walking back towards their car, pulling her towards him with the threat of the fallout of what was unfolding. The kind man who'd taken their photo looked at her with eyes full of sympathy, the awkward line of how much a stranger should intervene making him stop and recoil, suddenly unsure. Ida realised then – stood with damp clothes and dirty boots – that she was scared, and the man knew she was scared. They looked at each other, an offer of a way out suspended between them, then Ida turned and jogged towards Cal, towards his silence that would only last so long.

Walker left her to her thoughts for a while and Ida was grateful for it. She closed her eyes and breathed, trying to calm her racing mind. Eventually, he reached into the back seat and grabbed his backpack. 'I could do with a few things from inside,' he said. 'You want to wait here?'

Ida didn't respond; she didn't know what she wanted. She didn't want to go inside, nor did she want to wait alone in the car. She wanted to be back in her own little house in the middle of nowhere, living in the sweet comfort of ignorance. Ida knew the door this new world could open for her, the opportunities that were now available which she thought had passed her by. She could make amends with her sister. She could have a family of her own one day. She could get back to her career. Ida was able to talk herself through these new options but they didn't seem real. Nothing did.

When she didn't reply Walker spoke again, a calmness in his voice that Ida needed to hear. 'Shall we go back?' he asked.

She shook her head, staring at the door to the supermarket, her gaze fixed on the comings and goings. It didn't seem fair that people were just getting on with their life while hers had been paused for the past three years. Or maybe fair wasn't the right word – these people weren't responsible and they owed her nothing – but it just didn't seem *possible.*

'No, you go. I'll be okay here.' Ida reasoned that the discomfort of sitting in the truck alone would weigh less than the guilt of Walker leaving empty-handed. She'd feel as though she'd deprived him, and after everything he'd done for her she couldn't do that.

'Sure?'

'I'm sure.'

Walker got out of the truck and walked quickly into the shop, disappearing inside and leaving Ida sat alone. The keys were dangling from the ignition and for a fleeting moment Ida considered jumping into the driver's seat and speeding back towards the hills. The panic was still coming in waves, up and down, slow then fast. She wondered if she would ever feel normal again. Betrayal can do that to a person: it can make them question everything that ever was and continue to question everything that comes after. Ida felt as though Cal's lies had left a gaping hole in her chest where a fire now raged, angry and vengeful. The pain was as real as anything she'd ever felt before.

A van pulled up next to Ida, dirty and white with 'Clean Me' written on the dusty sides. A couple of men got out in thick yellow jackets and boots – workmen, Ida thought. She felt herself recoil as one of them squeezed past her, between the van and Walker's truck. She watched them walk into the shop, one of them chatting on his phone while the other opened the door, standing back to let a woman exit. She was pushing a pram, a blue-and-green toy hanging from the hood and shopping bags bulging in the basket.

Walker emerged less than five minutes later and Ida couldn't help but wonder whether he'd made sacrifices in order to get back to her; foregone some of the things he would usually stock up on in order to check she was still in one piece. She didn't like the idea of him thinking of her as fragile or broken. She'd grown accustomed to feeling like a stronger version of the Ida from before, independent and capable. She'd seen this new-found Ida reflected in Cal's eyes too. Several times she'd seen the surprise on his face when he'd found out something she'd overcome or discovered some new way in which she'd grown. Sometimes she'd wondered whether he'd expected her to fail, or at least to struggle more than she had, and whether he resented not being able to swoop in and save her. But the thoughts were always brief, barely settling before quickly being overshadowed by so many other things.

Walker opened the back door and put his bag on the seat, the zip struggling against the contents now stuffed inside. In his other hand was a big bottle of whisky which he placed on its side in the footwell. He got back in the truck, started the engine and eased out of the car park, driving back towards the hills.

CHAPTER TWENTY-TWO

They drove back in silence, Ida's mind too full of other things to talk, her brain trying to process the reality of what she'd seen. What should have been a lovely rural town, quaint and full of character, was actually the ugly and unquestionable confirmation of Cal's lies, and it made her chest burn with the fallout of his incomprehensible betrayal. She didn't understand *why*, and she couldn't imagine she ever would. Perhaps even Cal himself didn't.

Climbing Snowdon hadn't been the first time she'd seen him change that way – his emotions taking over, the Cal she knew slipping seamlessly into the shell of the man she loved. She'd lost count of how many times he'd tainted something that should have been a happy memory. It always started with his initial withdrawal, physically and emotionally, his stony silence and unwillingness to meet her eyes. The tension would simmer away, almost unbearable – Ida grew to think of it as the calm before the storm, knowing as time went on just how it would progress. Withholding his love from her was never enough.

Then the accusations – she'd been flirting with the man who'd taken their photo, making Cal feel small and pathetic;

she'd made a stressful experience all about her, never asking Cal how he felt or whether he was okay; he'd planned to propose at the top of the mountain but her selfish attitude had caused him to reconsider everything, to reconsider whether he wanted to be with her at all. The accusations always came thick and fast and somewhat chaotically, but she still wanted them to last, because while he was hurling insults and allegations at her he wasn't spiralling; he wasn't holding her up against the hotel wall by her throat or giving her bruises she would have to hide from everyone she loved.

Walker parked up by the road and Ida's seat belt was off and the door open before he'd turned off the engine. She jumped out and looked over towards the hills, knowing that on the other side stood some degree of comfort. She stood with her hands on her hips and tried to take it all in, listening to the birds and the river, the high-pitched songs mingled with the low rush of the water. She breathed it all in like a drug, as though her life depended on it. The air felt fresher here; she thought she could feel it cleansing her, rushing into her lungs and carrying out the smog of the town. In reality, Ida knew there was little smog in a small rural town like Hamilton, but she couldn't shake the feeling that she'd been contaminated by life; by the existence of *others*.

'You okay?' It was the first time Walker had spoken since before the supermarket, and his voice caught her by surprise, as though she'd forgotten he was there.

Ida nodded and swallowed hard, trying to gather herself. 'I'm okay.'

He slung the backpack over his shoulder and grabbed the bottle of whisky out of the truck.

'Better get back,' he said, using the bottle to point towards the setting sun to the west.

They walked up over the hill and, at the peak, Ida stopped to take in the view; she didn't have the luxury of seeing her little piece of the world from this height usually. She had begun to take the land for granted, the wonder and the beauty of it quickly becoming the norm, the impact of it tainted by the consistency of waking up to the same thing every morning. But now, as she stood watching the low sun reflecting in the river and the harshness of the land softening under the fading light, she realised how lucky she was.

Walker stood beside her and, glancing at him, she could tell that he was seeing the same thing she saw, the raw indisputable beauty rather than the bleak. He waited, letting her take the lead, knowing that she needed it. The wind was getting stronger, it blew through the forest and whipped at the water, howling as it became trapped between the hills. Ida pulled the zip up on her coat then set off down the hill, Walker just behind her.

When they neared the hut Walker let the backpack fall off his shoulder, carrying it in his hand as he made his way towards the door. Ida stopped, unsure what to do or where to go. The sun seemed to be setting the sky alight, a distant fire on the horizon behind the trees. Ida stood looking at it, torn between staying and leaving, unsure whether the former was an option. Part of her didn't want to go home – a bigger part of her than she was willing to admit – because she knew she would feel Cal's lies all the more there, where reminders of him littered her space, suffocating her.

Walker opened the door and Chief came bounding out, wagging his tail. Walker bent down on one knee and fussed him, his backpack on the floor next to him. He unzipped it and took out a clear plastic bag, passing him something from inside. 'Here you go, boy.' Chief took it and retreated happily back into the hut. Walker stood and turned to Ida. 'You coming?' He didn't wait for an answer, he just propped the door open with a rock and went back inside.

Ida stood and watched the sky change, the night taking over and putting out the fire. She felt herself relax; the sky had made her decision for her and given her an excuse. It would be easier to stay at Walker's now that the darkness had closed in, masking her path home.

Walker didn't say anything when she walked in, it was as though she belonged there and her presence required no comment. On the table by the window, Ida noticed a little pile of shopping. Among them, a pack of four cans of Coke and a box containing a chocolate fudge cake. She stood and traced her finger over the edges of the box, and then the cold aluminium of the cans. Other items were stacked among the Coke and the cake, things Ida hadn't seen in years. Bread. Bacon. A pack of chocolate digestives. A share-size bag of crisps. Brown sauce.

Walker appeared beside her. 'Let's have dinner first.' He took the bacon and wandered back outside.

Before long, Ida could smell the bacon cooking. She was like a moth to a flame, wandering outside to watch Walker hunched over the firepit with a pair of metal tongs in his hand. 'Won't be long,' he said. He walked back inside and returned a minute later with a couple of plates, the bread and the sauce.

Ida sat down on one of the chairs. 'Has anything changed... while I've been out here?'

Walker turned to face her. 'You mean out there?' He pointed over towards the hills with the tongs. 'Not really.' He shrugged. Ida wasn't sure if he'd tell her if anything had in fact changed, or whether he'd even know about it.

'How often do you go there?'

'Hamilton?' He turned back to the bacon and began taking it off the firepit and loading it onto the bread. 'Depends,' he said. 'Every few months, sometimes longer if I've managed to catch a lot of my own food.'

'But you go to the supermarket and stock up on things?'

'Sometimes. I'll buy bulk then leave it in the truck and walk back and forth to get it.'

'Why don't you use the dirt track?'

He thought about it for a moment, as though realising for the first time that this was an option. 'I don't want the temptation, I suppose.'

'The temptation?'

'Yeah, like with most things, if it's there, you'll use it. Parked over the hills, I almost forget about it. Besides, seems a shame to have a big ugly truck spoil my view.'

'Why do you live here?'

'You're full of questions all of a sudden,' he said, and Ida understood what he meant – this wasn't a topic for discussion, which only made Ida more curious. He passed her a plate with a bacon sandwich on it, as though it were the most ordinary thing he'd ever done. Ida stared blankly at it, trying to recall the last time she'd had bacon... or bread. He held out the bottle of brown sauce to her and she took it.

'Thank you.' Ida ate it greedily, barely taking a breath. When she looked up from her plate, Walker was stood with his half-eaten sandwich in his hand, looking down at her with a lopsided smile. 'What?' she asked.

'You like your food.'

'I've lived on rice for three years. I've missed good food.'

Walker's face dropped and she thought she could detect a hint of anger in his eyes. 'What's wrong?' she asked.

He took another bite of his sandwich and spoke with his mouth full. 'Just seems particularly cruel is all.'

'What does?'

'Imprisoning you with lies then depriving you of the things you enjoy.'

Ida looked down at her empty plate. It was as though she couldn't think too deeply about the enormity of Cal's deceit before something kicked in – a wall or a barrier of some kind, shutting her down, rendering her unable to process any more information.

Walker seemed to notice; he reached out and took the plate from her. 'Cake?' he asked.

'Yes,' Ida exhaled. 'Definitely cake.'

He disappeared into the hut but Chief remained outside; he looked at her for a while before making his way over and sitting by her side. She hesitated for a moment, her head telling her to hold back, but his eyes weakened her resolve and she reached her hand out and placed it on his head. Chief panted, his tongue out, then gradually began to lean against her legs. She'd always liked dogs; she'd broached the subject with Cal once, asking whether it might be good for her to have a little company. He'd tilted his head to one side and looked at her sceptically.

'Company? You mean like the chickens?' he'd said. And that had been the end of the subject – she didn't need any further reminders of her failures.

'Here we go.' Walker handed her a huge chunk of chocolate fudge cake – a quarter of the whole thing, she thought. Her instincts told her to have a smaller piece, to ration the luxury, but she quickly reminded herself that there were probably a million more pieces just like this one at a shop just over the hills.

'The last time I had chocolate cake was my birthday, just before we came here.' March twelfth, she reminded herself. They'd gone out for dinner to a nice restaurant in Surrey. She'd had steak and chips with a glass of wine then chocolate cake and cream for dessert. It had been just Ida and Cal; by that point, most of Ida's friends had stopped inviting her out – stopped checking in on her, even – and it had been months since her fallout with her sister. She'd isolated herself from everyone who loved her, because they could all see the things Ida couldn't.

They both sat eating their cake, Ida relishing the smooth,

chocolatey sweetness one mouthful after another. She almost couldn't finish it, her stomach was so full. She glanced over at Walker a couple of times between mouthfuls, wondering whether she should fill the silence that had settled between them, the darkness only emphasising that the two of them were very much alone. It didn't bother her, the quiet, and it didn't seem to bother Walker either, so she let it linger, wondering at what point Walker would turn in for the night, leaving her questioning what to do once more. After a while, when the creamy light of a half moon had begun to illuminate the river, Walker got up and stretched before disappearing inside and returning with a can of Coke and a bottle of whisky.

'Which do you prefer?' he asked.

Ida took the Coke, opening it and listening to the old familiar fizz. Walker unscrewed the lid from the whisky and drank a long gulp straight from the bottle before sitting back down heavily next to Ida and kicking off his boots. Ida copied, slipping off her boots and taking a sip from the can. It was sweeter than she remembered and it made her eyes tingle. Walker held the bottle out to her and she grabbed it, taking a drink and screwing up her face at the taste. It made her cough, the strength of it overpowering, but after the initial sting it petered off, leaving a nice warming sensation in her chest. She took another drink and passed it back.

They sat like that for a while, the bottle passing back and forth, the can of Coke long forgotten.

'So,' Walker said. 'You just need a bath.'

'Sorry?'

'You said music, cake, Coke and a bath...'

'Oh! Yes. That's right. A hot bath, with bubbles. And candles...' She took another swig from the bottle.

'Your list keeps growing.'

'Yours doesn't?'

'My list gets smaller.'

'Smaller than... ice?'

'I think ice will remain. But there used to be other things on that list.'

'Oh yeah, like what?'

He took a long drink and Ida saw from the light of the moon that the bottle was now half empty. Walker shrugged. 'Pizza.'

'Ah pizza, yes. I'll add that to my list. What else?'

'A fridge.'

Ida laughed. 'A fridge?'

Walker nodded. 'Stuff doesn't keep out here. Milk, cheese, cold beer.'

'Couldn't you have a little one? Run it off the solar panels.'

'I could, but...'

'But what?'

He took another drink, thinking. 'It might not make much sense to you, but I just don't want my life to get too comfortable out here.'

Ida frowned. 'Why?'

'Because I don't think I deserve it.'

Ida wasn't sure how to respond, but her gut told her not to push him for information she felt sure he didn't want to part with. 'I don't think you could call your life out here comfortable.'

Walker didn't reply, so Ida let it go, unspoken words escaping silently out into the night sky to sit among the canopy of stars. She took the bottle from Walker and drank.

Ida woke with a heavy head and a dry mouth – her first hangover in years. She struggled to open her eyes against the light, squinting and pulling a blanket up over her face, resenting the sun for rising and invading her sleep. They'd stumbled inside in the early hours, the whisky long gone and Chief already asleep on the floor. They'd collapsed on the bed in the clothes they were wearing and Ida had drifted into a comfortable sleep that defied the situation. It was the alcohol, she told herself. She would never have shared a bed with a man she barely knew if it weren't for the alcohol.

'Here,' said Walker, his voice low and gravelly. He cleared his throat and Ida lowered the blanket to look up at him. He was holding a mug out for her with steam rising from the top; she sat up and took it, smelling the rich aroma of the coffee.

'Thank you.' She tried to remember the details of the night before but her memory was hazy. She could recall chatting outside, and she could remember sitting in silence and drinking the whisky which burnt her throat and blurred her mind. 'My head's throbbing,' she groaned.

'We got through some whisky.'

'A whole bottle!'

'You got quite the taste for it.'

Ida pulled a face, remembering the smell which now turned her stomach.

'I'm cooking the rest of the bacon; it won't be a minute.'

Ida wasn't sure whether it would help settle her stomach or not. She sipped at her black coffee but it was still steaming and she couldn't gulp it down as quickly as she'd like. Her mouth was so dry, her tongue like sandpaper. Walker had drifted back outside, still in last night's clothes with his hair pulled back in a hair tie. She wondered how long he'd been up or whether he'd slept at all. 'Have you got any water?' she shouted out to him.

'Kitchen cupboard,' he replied.

She could smell the bacon cooking and her stomach grumbled in response – perhaps it would help after all. She got up and wandered over to the cupboards at the back of the hut –

there were only two of them. She opened the first and found that it was packed full of food – boxes, tins and bags. She opened the other and found the bottom shelf contained a good stash of beer, a bottle of rum and several bottles of water. She grabbed one, pulling it out of the cupboard, but as she did so something caught her eye. Stacked on the top shelf were several newspapers. She looked at them and frowned then glanced back over her shoulder. She could just see Walker prodding at the firepit.

She took the papers out and looked at the one on the top. It was the one Walker had shown her with the picture of the car accident on the front. She lay it on the counter and looked at the next one, holding it out in the light of the morning sun. On the front page was a picture of a woman smiling at the camera, a picture that warmed Ida's heart for a split second before it sent it into free fall. The woman's red hair fell below her shoulders, a thin trail of freckles standing out against her porcelain skin. She couldn't see it in the picture but Ida knew that, if she looked, there'd be a little butterfly tattoo at the top of her spine, a relic from her wild teenage years which she later grew to regret.

It was Maeve – Ida's sister.

CHAPTER TWENTY-THREE

Ida heard a noise behind her and turned to see Walker stood watching her, a look in his eyes that she hadn't seen before – Fear? Regret? Shame?

'You weren't meant to see those. At least, not yet.'

Ida didn't respond. She looked back to the paper, desperate for information. She'd seen the headline – had read it what seemed like a million times already – and yet she still didn't feel able to process what it meant. In search of clarity, she looked back at Walker.

'I'm sorry,' he whispered, his voice catching in his throat.

Ida was shaking her head, refusing to believe it. 'No. No, no, no...' Tears were falling freely, dripping onto the paper she held clutched in her hands.

Walker stepped closer to her and put his hands on her shoulders and, for a moment, Ida wondered whether he was going to shake her, to try and jolt her out of her refusal to believe what she had read. But he didn't. He took the newspaper from her and placed it on the counter with the others then he wrapped his arms around her, pulling her into him. She didn't hug him back but she let herself be held, the emotion pouring out of her while somehow remaining with her – she couldn't free it, she would never be able to free it. It was too much.

Walker held her, his strength making up for her lack of. She wept into his chest and shook with the grief that had taken hold of her. She wondered how she would ever feel anything but this pain again. She felt she had become it, defined by this void she would now carry with her for eternity.

Walker didn't speak or try to offer her words of condolence, and in that moment Ida knew: he understood this kind of pain. He'd lived it himself.

Eventually, with swollen eyes and a throbbing head, Ida pulled away. 'Why do you have this?' She pointed to the newspaper.

'That day,' Walker began. 'The day of the accident I told you about. The woman... that was your sister.'

Fresh tears began to fall. 'You... you *met* her?'

'She came looking for you.'

Ida turned away from him, her eyes blurred from the tears. She rubbed at them, then ran her fingers through her hair before turning back.

'You *spoke* to her?'

Walker nodded. 'Briefly. She was... she was injured. I stayed with her but she was in and out of consciousness. She kept saying she was looking for her sister, that *he'd* kept her sister away from her.'

'I can't believe she came looking for me.' Ida swallowed hard and wiped her eyes on the back of her sleeve. 'Did she say anything else?'

'She...' Walker bit his lip then put his head in his hands, taking a deep breath before answering. 'She asked me to find you. She asked me to make sure you were okay.'

'I'm... I'm... I'm not okay!' Ida raised her voice, angry at the unfairness of it all, the injustice of losing the two people she loved the most in the world in two entirely different ways.

'I know.' Walker stood watching her as she paced back and forth, but he didn't move; he just stood with his eyes on her, ready if she needed him.

'It's not fair!' she cried. 'Not Maeve.' She stopped suddenly and walked towards Walker. 'What about the girls?' Ida tried to calculate how old they'd be – Violet and Ivy, her little nieces. They must be seven now.

Walker took one of the papers from the pile and opened it, turning to a page part way through. 'There was a mention of them in here, on the day of her funeral. "Maeve McConnor leaves behind her husband, Reuben McConnor, and their children Violet and Ivy, seven".' Walker put down the newspaper and looked at Ida again. 'I assumed they were with their dad?'

Ida nodded; Reuben was a good man, a good father. The tears that fell down her cheeks were no longer for herself and the loss that she felt; they were for Violet and Ivy and their loss which seemed immeasurable. Her heart ached for them as she recalled the pain she felt at the loss of her own mother, the cancer which had slowly taken her from them too soon. Her death had accelerated the breakdown in Ida's relationship with Maeve. Fraught emotions and uncontrollable grief had made way for Cal to steer Ida away, to set her on a path of isolation, to control her under the guise of protection. She'd felt so vulnerable and Cal so strong – she'd relished his guidance, his security.

'Let's go for a walk,' Walker said quite suddenly. Ida was agitated, unable to keep still. She could tell that Walker wanted to help but he didn't really know how.

Ida didn't protest or agree, she just followed him aimlessly out of the hut, Chief at their heels. They headed out towards the river then followed it round until they came to a shallow section with a plank of wood stretching across it.

'You put this here?' Ida asked.

'Yep, when I first got here. Need the wood from the forest in the winter.' They crossed to the other side and skirted the treeline before entering the woodland via a narrow opening; there was no path as such but Ida could tell Walker had made this journey many times before, the ground was well trodden and the undergrowth separated where his boots had trampled.

Walker led the way, Ida behind and Chief trailing somewhere further back, sniffing at the tree trunks and finding his own path among the familiar woodland. Ida always had mixed feelings about the forest, it was so thick and dense that she couldn't see very far ahead. Sometimes, she felt protected; other times, she felt suffocated. The canopy blocked the view of the sky and brought its own atmosphere, cool and fresh, with the aroma of the rotting leaves underfoot, sweet and earthy.

They walked for a while, Ida losing track of time as she so often did out here. She hadn't been aware that they'd made any turns or arced to one side, but all of a sudden the trees gave way to the fields again, the riverbank just ahead. Somehow, while sheltered inside the forest, the burden she would have to live with had worked its way under her skin: her sister died trying to find her. She didn't know how she would ever make sense of that.

'I wonder if...' she began. They'd come out further down the river, where the banks swelled with the flow of the deeper waters. Walker didn't prompt her, he just waited for her to gather the words in her head before she spoke. 'I wonder whether Cal knows.'

'About your sister?'

'Well, everything.'

'I suspect he'll know about Maeve. I don't see how he could know about you figuring everything out.'

'Yes, that's what I was thinking.'

They followed the river back round to the crossing and Walker waited for Ida to step over first. Once on the other side he stopped and turned to her. 'I'm sorry I didn't help you sooner,' he said.

'I'm not your responsibility,' Ida said, blushing under the weight of his sudden honesty.

'I made a promise. To your sister. And I feel like I let her down.'

'You didn't owe her anything, you didn't even know her.'

'No, but when you make a promise to someone as their life is slipping away... you keep it.'

Ida looked down at the ground, fresh tears stinging her eyes. 'Did she know Cal was lying to me?'

Walker shook his head. 'I don't think she knew why you were out here, or what he'd told you, but she knew it wasn't good. That's the impression I got anyway.'

'What did he say to you that day, when I saw you talking to him?'

'He told me you'd had a breakdown and that I should keep away from you. He said you were unpredictable and prone to violence.'

Ida laughed at the absurdity of it all; she couldn't help it, she needed to mask the pain with something loud and all-consuming. She threw her head back and laughed up to the sky, her belly aching and her throat dry. Walker stood and observed her, this wild and grieving woman whose heart may be broken but was still strong. Her hair caught in the winds coming in off the hills, billowing around her as she became lost in a moment of sweet relief. They both knew it would only be temporary.

The denial lasted until Ida had no energy left to laugh in the face of Cal's absurdity. When it ended, she felt numb, as though she had been granted a momentary reprieve from feeling anything at all. She fell to the ground and sat there for a while – Walker next to her picking at the grass – listening to the sound of the river and watching as something scurried around among the ragged undergrowth at the treeline. A moment later, a pheasant appeared and in its wake, three babies, tiny and mottled with golden browns. Ida watched as the mother led them back into the safety of forest.

'I don't know what to do. I just... I have no idea where to start.'

Walker took a long, deep breath then threw the grass he'd picked onto the ground in front of him. 'What do you *want* to do?'

Ida thought about his question, really thought about what it was that she wanted to do. In time, she felt certain she would want to do *something*. Perhaps she would want answers, to understand why Cal had led her down this path and isolated her from everyone and everything; or perhaps she would want revenge. But for now, she felt she was doing exactly what she wanted to do in that moment: sat among the land she knew so well with the only friend she had left – if she could call him that.

'Right now? Nothing.'

Walker lay down on the grass and closed his eyes. 'Then that's exactly what we'll do.'

CHAPTER TWENTY-FOUR

I da felt detached from her emotions. She knew they were there, waiting for her, and she could identify them all quite clearly, but she couldn't *feel* them. She was numb, but she was aware that it wouldn't last. It couldn't. Part of her wanted to get on with it, to delve into the grief and the anger head first. She knew that what she was feeling now – although preferable to feeling what was waiting for her – could only ever be temporary, but she accepted that it's what her mind needed before succumbing to the inevitable pain. The calm before the storm.

Ida spent several days suspended in that emotionless state. She didn't go home and neither she nor Walker put up the pretence that it was an option. Ida couldn't face going back there and Walker didn't want her to leave. Nothing happened between them. Walker had progressed from sleeping on the floor to spending his nights in a hammock outside. The nights were getting warmer and he never seemed to sleep much anyway. They got along, never talking much but enjoying each other's company. Ida thought that he was the closest thing she'd had to a friend for a long time.

She'd had a good group of friends once, before she met

Cal. Her best friend, Ellen, had tried to keep in touch for longer than the rest, but sooner or later even she'd relented, retreating into the shadows never to be seen again. Ida couldn't blame her, there were only so many times you could make excuses or avoid someone before it became obvious. One evening, just before Christmas, Ellen had turned up at her house carrying a large gift-wrapped present and a bottle of wine. Ida had been in the bedroom and could see her coming, walking down the street in a long fur coat and scarf, her short black bob gleaming under the street lights. Ida felt her shoulders tense. Cal had just got out of the shower; they were going out for a meal to a local Italian restaurant and Ida was half ready, her hair and make-up done but still dressed in her robe. Cal had walked over to her with a towel tied around his waist, embracing her from behind as she looked out of the window between a narrow gap in the curtains. Cal followed her gaze.

'Did you know she was coming?'

'No, I had no idea.'

'If you'd rather go out with Ellen I can cancel our reservations.'

'No, no, of course I wouldn't rather go out with her.'

He'd moved her hair out of the way and began kissing her neck. Ida resisted at first, sidetracked by wanting to speak to her friend but not wanting to upset her boyfriend, then she heard Cal inhale sharply and hold his breath for a moment before letting it go. She could feel the warmth on her neck.

'Are you sure?'

'I'm positive.'

She knew things were better between them when it was just the two of them with nothing to distract or cause another argument. Cal had spun her round and allowed his towel to fall to the floor. As they heard a knock on the door he pulled her into him, smiling, with a glint in his eye which told her she'd said the right thing.

———

Ida lost count of how long it had been since she'd hit the pause button on life. She wondered how much longer it would last; how many more minutes or hours or days until it all came crashing down around her.

One night, in the early hours, she got her answer. She woke to the darkness and, for the first time, she *felt* her sister's absence. It was as though she'd had some part of herself removed; one minute it was there, the next it was gone. She ran out into the night and wailed, a primal howl that woke Walker from a dreamless sleep. Ida fell to her knees out in the fields as though she were praying to the moon, a crumbling silhouette highlighted by its translucent light.

Walker didn't intrude on her grief; he gave her the space she needed to be vulnerable. It took a certain type of strength for her to allow herself to feel this way, even if she didn't realise it. She stayed like that for some time, her cries carried into the night until she could cry no more. She lay down among the coarse grass, exhausted, and Walker got up from his hammock and followed the path she'd taken out into the field. She'd curled up in the foetal position, her hair covering her face and her hands clasped to her chest. She was still crying but it was more of a whimper than a sob; a cry that had lost its steam. Walker sat down beside her.

'Tell me about her.'

Ida sat up slowly, pushing her hair back off her face and looking up at the night sky. 'She was older than me. Almost two years, but the gap always seemed so much bigger really. She married young and had twin girls. She took care of our mother when she was sick, in ways I just wasn't able to. Then she took care of me when Mum died – or at least she tried to. She was a veterinary nurse – she loved animals, especially dogs. She had a chocolate Labrador called Everest – the girls were *obsessed* with *PAW Patrol*.'

Walker didn't say anything, he just let her talk about her sister, telling him things she forgot she remembered.

'When we were little, she used to say we carried a little fire inside of us because of our red hair. She'd say we had to keep our fire burning so we could do anything we wanted in life, because no one messes with fire.' Ida laughed as the tears fell, the moonlight reflecting in the damp trails they left on her cheeks.

Walker smiled. 'I think she was right. I think you do have a fire burning inside – I see it in your eyes as well as in your hair.'

They sat and watched the stars travel, the skies changing as the world continued to turn.

'She was right about him,' Ida whispered, unsure whether she wanted Walker to hear. He turned to look at her but didn't say anything, his eyes encouraging her to go on. 'Maeve was right about Cal. She was right all along.'

'She didn't like him?'

Ida shook her head. 'Maeve saw the good in everyone. Our dad left when we were really young – I can't remember him at all but Maeve always said he was a nice man who had his own reasons for leaving. It used to really annoy me that she could choose to see the good in a man who had abandoned his family. She said you couldn't judge someone without knowing their reasons. But with Cal... she *hated* him. I tried to tell her that he had his reasons for being so... so...' she thought for a moment, trying to find the right words, 'controlling and manipulating and jealous...' She found that once she started listing his traits she couldn't stop. 'He'd been cheated on before – or so he said – so he had trust issues. Maeve said that was bullshit. She said he had mean eyes and a cruel heart.'

Walker was watching her talk, his eyes fixed on her mouth. It felt almost intimate, the way he seemed so lost in her.

'I should have listened to her,' Ida said. 'I should have known she was looking out for me; that's what she always did.'

Walker turned away from her now and looked back up to the stars.

'Maeve sounds very wise, but love can blind you.'

Not for the first time, Ida felt herself on the cusp of a conversation Walker was reluctant to have. She wondered whether he was speaking from experience but she didn't want to ask him anything about himself only to be shut down again; it felt like she would be giving a little piece of herself away, letting him know she was interested in parts of him he could not share. As the sun began to rise to the east, a pink tinge on the horizon, Ida's eyes became heavy and dry. She yawned, suddenly exhausted.

'Come on, let's get some sleep.' He stood and held out his hand and Ida looked at him, this tall figure of a man with all the hair. She thought how little she knew him; how he let her into his physical world so unquestioningly yet closed off the rest entirely. It was the opposite for Ida, she had little to offer physically yet Walker seemed to know so much about her life. It made her feel vulnerable and exposed at times, the imbalance. But other times she saw it as even – they both gave whatever they could.

Ida reached out and took his hand.

CHAPTER TWENTY-FIVE

A month passed, time slipping by without declaring itself, just a series of hours and days and weeks. Walker had watched Ida read the newspaper articles and then reread them many times, always returning them – neatly folded – to the cupboard afterwards, only to be looked at again hours or days later. She hadn't cried again after that night out in the field, it was as though she was out of tears. Walker stood by her when she needed him and left her alone when she didn't; it was as though he knew what was best for her even when she didn't.

Maeve had been going too fast – or so the papers said. She wasn't used to the winding, narrow roads of the country and the tight corner had taken her by surprise. She'd lost control and crashed head-on into a Land Rover which had careered off of the road relatively unscathed. Maeve's little white hatchback had flipped, landing upside down at the base of an alder tree. Walker had been heading to his truck nearby when it had happened and he ran over to try to help. The driver of the Land Rover was in shock. 'She came out of nowhere,' he kept repeating, staring at Walker, looking for the type of reassurance that he was unable to give; he wanted to hear it wasn't his fault and, later, he probably would, but at that moment Walker couldn't care less about attributing blame. The man's nose was bleeding where he'd hit the airbags and he was holding his arm at a funny angle, his right hand cupping his left elbow.

Walker had told him to call for help but he'd just stood, trembling and useless. 'She came out of nowhere. I didn't see... She just came out of nowhere.' Walker had felt the man's pockets and found his phone tucked inside. He'd called 999 and directed them the best he could – it would have to be the air ambulance, they'd said. He couldn't open the door to the white hatchback which had sustained considerable damage, but the passenger side window had smashed so he climbed half in, telling the woman he found there that help was on its way.

She was bleeding from her head and her mouth as she hung upside down, restrained by the seat belt, her hair hanging limply beneath her. The airbags had deployed and were smeared with blood, filling the space between Maeve and the steering wheel. Walker struggled against the one in the passenger side, slipping through the gap to take her hand. She was falling in and out of consciousness. Walker stayed with her, talking to her about things he could barely recall; things that mattered as much as they didn't. He tried to keep her from sleep or whatever else waited for her behind closed eyes.

'My sister,' she'd said. 'She's out here.'

'Your sister?'

'Please, help her. Please.'

'Where is she?' For a moment, Walker had thought that someone else had been in the car, that she'd been thrown through the window screen and lay somewhere on the road – but the window was still there, shattered but intact.

'Out there, somewhere.' Maeve had pointed limply over beyond the hills and Walker had understood: the woman with the wild red hair much like this woman's. The woman who lived in solitary, visited infrequently by the man with the truck full of food. 'He... he kept her... kept her from me,' Maeve had whispered. 'Don't... trust... him...'

Maeve's hand stopped trembling and her shallow breaths began to fade away. The helicopter hovered above, the winds whipping at the grassland as it landed.

'Stay with me.' He'd held her hand tighter as though trying to hold on to the life that had begun to slip away. 'Help is here, just hold on.'

'Promise... me...' she'd breathed, blood gurgling in her mouth and distorting her words. 'Promise you'll fi... find her.'

'I promise,' Walker replied.

He withdrew from the car to greet the doctor running from the helicopter, and as the gusts from the propellers thrashed at his face, he told himself it was their force that had caused the tears to pool in his eyes; tears he had not felt in a long time.

It had been a warm, dry summer. The heat had brought a couple more storms and, after each one, they'd walked to Ida's house to check on the roof. Each time, she'd collected a few more of her possessions and moved them wordlessly back to Walker's. She'd taken her list of sounds and her jigsaws, her favourite books and a bag full of clothes. She didn't see it as moving in with him, and neither did Walker, it was just a temporary arrangement that suited them both for the time being, while Ida recovered from the wounds no one could see and Walker learned to let his guard down, one day at a time.

It was late morning and Ida had joined Walker in the river, swimming against the current. She swam most days now and enjoyed long walks with Chief, collecting wood or exploring the areas she'd once considered out of bounds. She felt the physical strength she gained making up for her emotional weakness, her muscles stepping in where her mind could not. She hadn't been back to Hamilton but Walker had; he'd disappeared one morning and returned with the things he knew Ida liked most, not bothering to wake and ask her if she'd like to go, knowing that she wouldn't.

He'd bought her sausages and mustard and they'd had a barbeque at sunset, accompanied by another one of his purchases – a bottle of Southern Comfort. They'd drank too much and shared a moment Ida had wondered whether she'd imagined the following morning – their hands grazing under the moonlight, a look before they went to bed that made Ida wonder whether there was something there – something other than the companionship she'd told herself they both found solace in. The following morning was like nothing had happened – leftover sausage sandwiches outside the hut with the usual small talk they'd grown accustomed to. She'd put it out of her mind, and her heart, and enjoyed the simplicity of an uncomplicated friendship instead – if it could be called that.

She climbed out of the river and onto the grassy bank, Chief waiting as he always did. She'd once asked Walker why Chief never went for a swim. They were in the river, treading water as Chief lay watching them from the bank. Walker had thought about it for a moment as though he might have forgotten, then he looked over at Chief and said: 'I trained him not to. I'm not sure he'd be able to get back out himself and the current can get pretty rough.' It had made Ida smile, the way he spoke about his dog. Walker was still swimming as Ida dried herself, disappearing under the steady flow of the water and reappearing several metres away. As Ida tied the towel around her waist she heard a noise to the right – familiar yet alarming. It was a truck. Cal's.

She'd known he would return sooner or later, but she hadn't

expected him for at least another month and she had counted on that time to make a decision – would she hide from him? If not, what would she say?

Walker was suddenly beside her, his hair tied back off his face and his chest brown from the sun. He followed Ida's gaze to the truck in the distance then picked up his towel, rubbing his face before looking at her. He didn't speak, he simply waited for her to process what was happening and let him know what she needed. She could feel her heart hammering in her chest as though it was trying to escape. She could just make out Cal's silhouette as he climbed out of the car. Ida ran back to the hut. Inside, among her pile of things which Walker had put into a box, she found the binoculars. She took them back outside and pointed them in Cal's direction, through a gap in the trees. He was leaning against the truck with his hand to his ear and it took her a while to realise what he was doing – he was on the phone. Ida felt sick. She remembered her own mobile phone, the one Cal had taken with him one day, what seemed like a lifetime ago; the one he had returned without. *Phones are useless now, Ida.* Her jaw tensed as she remembered, then her neck and her shoulders; her whole body. Cal had told her they used long distance walkie-talkies to communicate now; that the mobile networks had gone down soon after the electrical grid. The effort of holding in the anger was causing Ida physical pain; a burden she knew she would only be able to carry for so long.

She carried on watching Cal, the way he leant casually against the driver's side door as though he didn't have a care in the world. Perhaps he didn't.

'He's on the phone,' Ida said.

Walker turned to look in Cal's direction, water dripping from his shorts. Ida could tell he wanted to say something but was holding back his words. He did this sometimes, restrained himself in a way that made Ida sure he'd learned to be this way

– a habit he was struggling to break. She lowered the binoculars and looked at him, waiting for him to ask her to stay. Instead, he turned round and walked into the hut.

Ida was torn. She stood in a moment of indecision, pulled in two separate directions. She wanted to run across the grassland and right into Cal. She wanted to tell him she knew everything; that she wasn't as stupid or naïve as he'd thought. She wanted to hurt him, physically and emotionally, and demand an explanation. She looked over her shoulder, in the opposite direction to Cal, towards the man with whom she'd sought refuge; the man who'd held her in his arms as she cried; who'd given up his bed for her to sleep in; who'd provided her with a safe space where she could grieve. She took a deep breath and ran her fingers through her hair, then she stormed into the hut.

Walker had changed into a dry pair of shorts and was rummaging through one of the cupboards.

'Aren't you going to say anything?' Ida asked him. She felt unsure of herself all of a sudden – unsure of the blurred lines between them and the boundaries they'd never set. They'd existed together entirely platonically, never needing or wanting anything more from each other than a chance to be human, to exist in their own varying emotions without judgement. Now here she was, suggesting there should be *something* from Walker, a reaction of some sort based on Cal's arrival. She couldn't decide what she wanted or expected from him, but she felt sure there should definitely be *something*.

'What do you want me to say?' he asked. He opened a bottle of water and took a long drink, wiping his mouth with the back of his hand when he'd finished. 'You know you can stay here,' he said, but he couldn't meet her eyes. Instead, he busied himself with tidying things he usually left, folding clothes that didn't need to be folded.

'You've never even asked me my name.' Ida had wanted to

say something for weeks; she didn't know why it irked her so much, but it just seemed wrong. She couldn't work out why he didn't seem to mind someone living in his hut whose name he did not know. Walker looked at her and shrugged nonchalantly. 'You don't even know me,' she said. She could feel all the things that had sat in the shadows now coming to the surface. 'You let me live here and I... I don't even know if you want me to or whether you just pity me. You cook for me but you don't even know my name or tell me why you're here.' Walker shifted on his feet looking uncomfortable with the conversation but Ida didn't care. 'You let me sleep in your bed and use your things but you won't even tell me your name. I don't know what I'm supposed to do!' She wasn't making sense, she knew that, but she couldn't help herself.

Walker frowned at her, confused. 'I can't tell you what to do.'

'Why?'

'Because I can't be the reason you stay.'

Ida felt out of breath, her heart was drumming so loudly she could hear it in her ears and feel it in her throat. 'Why not?' she asked. 'What would be so bad about that?' He looked down at the floor and sighed. Chief positioned himself between them as though making a point not to take sides. Walker looked back up at Ida but didn't say anything. 'Just talk to me. Just tell me what's going on here,' Ida pleaded. She felt a sudden sense of urgency that she hadn't felt before with Walker. He'd been so consistently there for her that she hadn't asked for anything more. She'd been intrigued but didn't feel in any rush to understand him or push him to talk about the things he was obviously protecting. But now, with Cal on his way to the house they'd once shared, she felt rushed. She didn't know what to do but she felt a need to understand Walker, to feel part of something which would anchor her.

Walker held his arms out to the side, exasperated, as though she was asking him for the impossible. Ida nodded. 'Right,' she said. 'I'd better go then.'

She turned to leave, deciding not to take her things – it would only stall her momentum and she needed that. As she stepped outside she thought she could hear Walker begin to say something, but when she looked back over her shoulder she saw that he was already looking the other way.

CHAPTER TWENTY-SIX

Ida had hoped Walker would call her back with answers to all of her questions. Tears welled in her eyes – angry, frustrated tears, tinged with the hurt she was reluctant to admit she felt. She knew he didn't owe her anything, he'd already given her so much, but it didn't make her feel any better that he was so unwilling to give her something that would cost him nothing – answers. Information. She didn't need a lot, just enough to understand him the way he did her.

She felt there was an imbalance – Walker knowing so much about Ida while she was flying blind. When she was upset, he understood it was because she was grieving for her sister. When she was apprehensive about going into town and seeing other people, he knew it was because she'd grown so distrusting of others. Whereas when Walker was staring into the distance, looking into memories that made his eyes glisten in the sunlight, Ida had no idea about the things he was seeing. She wanted to understand and, with a jolt to her heart, she realised it was because she cared. She wanted to be able to comfort him the way he had comforted her.

She walked slowly towards Cal's truck, allowing time for

Walker to catch up while knowing that he wouldn't. She thought enough time had passed that Cal would be on his way to the house now, supplies in his hands and tales of an imaginary world in his head. As she got closer to the truck she could see that it stood alone with no sign of Cal or his lies. She tried to open the door, hoping he would have left it unlocked although knowing that he wouldn't – it was too full of supplies; rations too scarce to risk being stolen, according to Cal. She rolled her eyes at the thought. She glanced back towards Walker's hut, hidden behind the trees and the shrubbery, then she turned round and set off towards the house.

She walked slowly, in no particular hurry to come face to face with Cal – her keeper, the man who had trapped her with a fear she did not need to feel. She hadn't worked out what to say or do and every time she tried to formulate a plan she found her brain unwilling to participate. The sun was high and bright in the sky, a warm golden glow bathing her path as Ida walked to the house, yellow gorse bushes and patches of holly interspersed among the long grass which reached her waist in some parts. Insects were alive with the air of summer, bees and butterflies and everything in between contributing to the wilderness that Ida called home. Ida was watching them when she heard the familiar voice calling her name; the voice which usually made her heart flutter for very different reasons.

She looked up to see Cal running towards her. She didn't react, she just stood watching him get closer and closer until she could see the look of horror on his face – a look which was no doubt reflected on her own.

'Ida, baby, are you okay? I was so worried about you.' He spoke quickly, out of breath and wide-eyed. Ida didn't respond so Cal took her in his arms and kissed her head repeatedly. 'What happened?' He took a step back and regarded her with concern – it made her feel sick, the emptiness of it. 'Ida?'

'There was a storm. Several, actually.'

'Jesus.' He rubbed at his jawline with his hand. 'Are you hurt?' Ida shook her head. To his credit, he was a good actor. The concern in his eyes, the compassion when he spoke, the relief that she hadn't been hurt... it all looked genuine. 'How did you fix the roof?' It was the question she'd been dreading. She hadn't decided whether she would confront Cal now or later; whether she would search for information or give him the opportunity to tell her himself, but whatever she decided, she knew she didn't want to involve Walker.

'I found the tarp in the forest a few weeks ago and brought it back here; I thought it might come in useful.' She'd made her decision without realising – to delay the inevitable truth. 'I found some nails and a hammer in the toolbox.' She shrugged nonchalantly as though it were of no real significance. Ida wasn't sure whether he looked impressed by her alleged resilience or insulted by it.

'That's... that's great, Ida. You did good.' He ran his fingers through his hair and looked over his shoulder towards the house then back to Ida. 'Shall we go in?' Ida nodded. 'I'll have a proper look at the roof but it looks like I'll need to source some materials and come back to fix it. What about the generator? Is it still working okay?'

Ida hadn't used it since before the storm; she'd had no need to. Walker had cooked on the firepit and they'd used the solar-generated electricity whenever they'd needed it, which much more infrequently than Ida had used the little red generator.

'Haven't used it since the last storm. It was wet through.'

'When was that?'

'Last week,' Ida lied.

'Last week? Are you sure?' Cal's voice was sceptical and the reality suddenly dawned on Ida that he would have been able to access weather reports – he would have known when the storms were coming. She wondered if that's why he'd arrived earlier than expected, to check on her. It was a little too late now, she thought.

'Positive.' She saw Cal's eyes narrow in confusion and she couldn't help but take pleasure in the fact that he would be unable to argue without revealing the truth; how else would he explain his sudden knowledge of the weather in an area he wasn't in? 'Why?'

'Just... we didn't have them in London.'

'That's a long way from here,' Ida said.

Ida hadn't thought about Cal as much as she would have expected to. Maeve's passing had consumed her and allowed little room for the anger she knew she should feel towards Cal – he'd robbed her of having a relationship with her sister for the past three years, and another year before they'd moved out here. They'd lost touch because of Cal's interference and how difficult he'd made their relationship. Maeve wouldn't have even been out here on unfamiliar roads if it wasn't for Cal. She felt a sudden lurch to her stomach at this thought and she had to swallow down the sudden urge to run away, to leave him in their broken home by himself, confused and without answers.

'Are you okay? You seem a bit quiet. Aren't you pleased to see me?'

'I... I wasn't expecting you yet.'

'Oh. Well, I can go if you'd prefer...' Cal gave her a half smile which told her it could go either way depending on her response. She didn't want to ask him to stay; she didn't want to satisfy his cruel need for control or beg him for his affection. But she didn't want him to go either. She didn't want to have to rush the revelation that she knew the truth.

'I'm just in shock. The storm and everything that followed.

The house flooded, my things were wet through. I haven't slept properly in days.'

He brushed his hand against her cheek. 'Where were you?' he asked, and she noticed his eyes flicked into the distance, towards Walker's place.

'I'd been for a walk.'

'North?' he asked.

'Through the forest then back along the river. I must have just missed you driving in.'

'I've told you not to wander too far, it's not safe. That weirdo lives down there.' He gestured out towards the hills with a look of disgust on his face.

They reached the house and Cal stood back, looking up at the roof. Ida wanted to tell him that that *weirdo* stepped in when he wasn't there; he cared for her and fed her while Cal was living his own life, entirely absent from hers for reasons she didn't yet understand.

'You seen him around here again?' he asked.

'Who? The man with the dog?'

'Yes, who else?'

'No. I haven't seen him.'

Ida could tell Cal was in a mood because he hadn't got the welcome greeting he'd come to expect; he revelled in her desperation to see him, she could see that now – the look of glee in his eyes as she ran towards him, the way he would withhold himself from her just enough to leave her craving his touch. Cal was an expert at turning up unannounced and making it seem as though he was doing her a favour. It reminded her of countless occasions before all of this, before he moved her away from everyone and everything.

She could remember her sister's thirtieth birthday. They'd gone on a girls' night out in London and had booked a hotel for the night. The twins were still young but old enough that Maeve was ready to spread her wings a little and spend the night away from them. There were eight of them in total, a mix of family and friends. Ida hadn't seen most of them since she started dating Cal.

Their cousin Maddie had booked them a table at a cocktail bar and by the time they got there they were all tipsy and laughing, enjoying their girls' night away from home. Ida was stood ordering drinks from the bar when she felt a hand clasp her wrist; it made her flinch.

'Baby, you're drunk. Let me take you home.'

Ida turned to find Cal stood next to her, his jaw clenched and his eyes narrowing, waiting for her response.

'Cal, what are you doing here?'

'What am *I* doing? I've come to check on you and that's the thanks that I get?'

'But I don't need you to check on me, I'm fine. I'm having a good time.'

Cal scoffed. 'You're making a fool of yourself, you can hardly walk.'

'Ida?' Maeve was at her other side now, her hand protectively placed around her waist. Ida noticed Cal's hand was still gripped tightly round her wrist. 'Callum, what are you doing here? It's my birthday, Ida is celebrating with us.'

Cal rolled his eyes. 'Are you going to let her talk to me like that?'

Ida looked from Cal to Maeve and back again, torn between the two people she loved most in the world.

'Ida, you don't have to go with him. You don't have to do what he tells you, it's not right.'

'Seriously, Ida, are you going to just stand there and let her speak to me that way after everything I've done for you?'

'Cal, I just want to celebrate with...'

He interrupted: 'She's never liked me! You know she's trying to tear us apart!'

Maeve laughed, a forced, angry laugh that caught Ida by surprise. 'Callum, leave us alone. Leave *Ida* alone. This isn't right, can't you see what you're doing to her?'

'What *I'm* doing to her? You pushed her out when her mum was dying so she never even got a chance to say goodbye.'

'What the hell? That's ridiculous. Ida, come and sit down.'

'Ida, you know she's trying to control you. Look at her, pulling at your arm. Your mum would want you to stand up for yourself.'

Ida had wanted to run away. She'd wanted to run into the night without looking back and find a place where she could hide from everything. She didn't know the right answer; she didn't know what she was supposed to do or who was right and who was wrong. She was overloaded with conflicting information. Did Maeve push her out? Were those her words or Cal's? Maeve had certainly taken the lead with caring for their mum but she felt sure that was because she'd found it too difficult to watch the strongest woman she knew fading away day after day. Maeve had never stopped her from seeing her mum, had she? She couldn't think straight.

'Come on, baby. Let me take you home.' Cal gently pulled on her arm and Ida felt herself going with him, her body making the decision her brain could not.

'Ida!' Maeve shouted after her, begging her to stay, but it didn't take long for the music to drown out her pleas.

When they got outside Cal let go of her arm and walked ahead, silent until they got to the corner of the road where the crowds thinned. Then he turned to her, his eyes full of a hate she didn't think she deserved, and spat on the floor right in front of her feet. 'You *ever* disrespect me like that again, Ida, and we're done.'

Two days later, after going on a bender with his friends, Cal came home drunk and punched her so hard the skin on her cheek split open. Ida apologised, because it was easier that way, and maybe she had disrespected him; she couldn't quite remember her exact wording of the things she'd said to him at the bar but Cal seemed to recall everything. Maybe she *was* drunker than she'd realised.

A week later, she spoke to her sister for the last time, a tearful phone call telling her not to contact her, her heart breaking into a thousand pieces, never to be whole again.

CHAPTER TWENTY-SEVEN

C al had surveyed the damage to the house, checking the roof with a scrutiny Ida felt sure was due to his desire to find something wrong; to pick fault with what he believed she'd done by herself.

'Probably could have done with being a bit tighter; don't want any rain getting in.'

'It's held well,' she commented.

He looked at her questioningly, his eyebrows raised, as though daring her to go on. Ida looked away.

'Where are all your things?'

Ida shrugged. 'Everywhere really, most were ruined.'

She held her breath, hoping he didn't press her further, and was relieved when he changed the subject. 'Vegetable patch doing okay?'

'Not really. The storm flooded it.' It was true, to a degree. It could have been saved, but she didn't have the inclination to tend to it the same as she had before, when she thought her life depended on it.

'Okay, I'll have to see if we can spare some supplies from the base; some fresh produce.'

'How are things going there?' Ida was curious, wanting to hear his latest lies almost as much as when she believed they were the truth.

'Not great. It's dreadful, actually, but we're doing what we can to help. I just hope it's enough.'

Ida had to turn away from him, she couldn't look him in the eye as he spoke; his pained expression was stirring a rage in her that she hadn't felt before. Had he always been this good an actor? Or had he got better with practice?

'What about Maeve?' Ida spoke quickly, forcing the words out without looking at him and then catching her breath so that it didn't betray her resolve.

'I'm trying, I really am.' He sat down at the kitchen table and sighed heavily. 'There are so many people and no system for keeping track of them anymore. It's like trying to find a needle in a haystack.'

'But you said there weren't many people left?'

'No,' he said slowly. 'But it's still a lot of people when you're trying to find just one.'

Ida walked over to the kitchen and looked out of the window, unsure where to go or what to do. She wanted to put as much distance between them as possible without him suspecting there was anything wrong.

'Don't you think I'm trying hard enough, is that what it is?'

'No. I just... I miss my sister.' The words hurt her to say.

'I know you do, and that's why I go back to that hell – for you. To try and find your sister and the girls. I know how important they are to you.'

Ida bit her lip and she felt her nostrils flare in anger. It was something Maeve always used to comment on – *Ida's angry... look at her nose!* She gripped the edge of the kitchen worktop until her knuckles turned white. 'There been a lot of planes flying over this past month or so.' She realised she was goading him, trying to trip him up or lead him into an area he couldn't explain. 'More than usual.'

'I know, baby. We're busy trying to keep the world ticking over.'

'Do you think she's still alive?' She spun round and looked right into his eyes, holding his gaze despite it making her feel sick to her stomach – she wanted to see deep into his soul, through the lies and the deceit. Did he know? If he did, he didn't show it.

'We have to believe she is, Ida, don't we? We have to have hope.'

Ida turned away from him again, pretending to busy herself at the kitchen sink. She looked out through the window and into the forest and found that her thoughts soon drifted to Walker. Was he out there? Was he thinking about her as she was him?

Cal walked over and slipped his arms around her waist, startling her. His mouth found her neck and his kisses sent shivers of repulsion down her spine. 'I'll go and take a look at the generator.' He disappeared outside and Ida's legs gave way. She dropped to the floor and brought her knees up to her chest, hugging them close to her body and closing her eyes shut tight. It was as though the Cal she thought she knew had left her the last time he was here and a different person had returned – a stranger, cold and hollow. She questioned herself; had he always been this way? Surely she couldn't have been this blind? It was so obvious to her now, the control and manipulation; the type of person he was and the type that he wasn't.

She remembered her last conversation with Maeve, tears streaming down her cheeks as she spoke into the phone, Cal watching her from the sofa though he was trying hard to feign disinterest.

'Ida, listen to me. I have always looked out for you, I have always loved you. You are blind when it comes to Callum. Open your eyes and you will see him for who he really is.'

'Goodbye, Maeve.'

'Ida, don't do this... do not let him...'

Ida hung up the phone and left the room. She didn't want Cal to see her cry, she felt that they were *her* tears and no one else's, and she should be allowed a moment of pure anguish by herself. As she walked to the bedroom, she heard Cal shout after her.

'For what it's worth, I support your decision.'

Had it been her decision? She wasn't sure; she wasn't sure about anything anymore.

'Generator's working fine.' Cal walked back into the house to find Ida still sat on the kitchen floor, her head resting against the cupboard. She saw a momentary look of disgust flit across his face as he watched her, as though he was repulsed by her show of weakness; she wouldn't have noticed it before, it was so fleeting it was almost imperceptible. Almost. He quickly reset, his eyes brimming with concern. 'Baby, what's wrong?'

'I'm just tired,' she said, getting to her feet. 'I think I'm going to go and have a lie down.'

'Good idea, I think I'll join you – I'm shattered after the long drive.' He followed her into the bedroom, Ida suddenly regretting her words. 'We'll have a nap then we'd better go and fetch the rest of the supplies.'

'Of course, the supplies. We can go and get them now, I'll sleep later...' She needed to put some physical distance between them, an empty space for her revulsion to fall; she felt sure that if he came too close he would sense it.

'Don't be silly, you need some rest. Come on.' He put his

hands firmly on her shoulders and guided her to the bed. She climbed in and pulled a sheet over her despite the warmth in the room. She hoped it would be another barrier between them, as though the emotional ones were not enough. She turned to face the wall, away from Cal, and she felt his arm wrap around her waist, finding its way under her T-shirt where his thumb began rubbing against her ribs.

Ida had never felt more awake. She lay staring at the wall, looking at the hairline cracks in the pastel-green paint; the way it had begun to flake onto the floor. After a while, Cal's arm became heavy and limp. His thumb stopped stroking her skin. His breathing became deep and heavy. She turned slowly to look at the ceiling, testing the limits of his sleep: would he feel her movement? To Ida's relief, he didn't stir. Slowly, she moved his arm off of her body and lowered it to his side, then she pulled the sheet off herself and quietly sat up. When her feet touched the floor she carefully stood, turning to check she hadn't disturbed him. He was still fast asleep, tired from the long drive and the web of lies he'd spun to get here.

She found his backpack propped against the back of the sofa. She unzipped it, her eyes darting back to the bedroom door as her heart pounded in her chest. In one of the side pockets she found what she was looking for – the keys to his truck. She wasn't sure why she wanted them, she hadn't had a conversation with herself about what she expected to find or why she needed to search it, she just felt that she *should*. There weren't many options and his truck was the one place she didn't usually go. Now that she thought about it, even when she went with him to collect supplies, he always passed them to her – she never set foot inside the interior.

She stood at the front door with the keys in her hand, suddenly unsure of herself; if Cal woke and found her gone he would come looking for her. She could just say she was trying to help by fetching some of the supplies while he rested, but she would still need to be careful – if he managed to creep up on her while she was searching it would be difficult to explain. Her stomach fluttered with anticipation and dread at what she might find. She knew what she wanted: some irrefutable evidence she could present to him to fast-track the denial and the additional lies which would inevitably come without proof. She could show him the book – *The Quiet Space Between Us* – but she knew that anything that had come from Walker would be scoffed at. She could hear him now: *The weirdo from the hut? You're going to take his word over mine?* She didn't want to feel as she always had before, questioning her own reality. If she told him she'd been into town, he would find some reason to explain why there was a thriving community in the countryside – an isolated zone which still wasn't safe for Ida or a camp for military personnel. The truth was, without physical, irrefutable evidence, she didn't trust herself not to believe more of his lies; not to be made to question what she knew to be true.

Slowly, she opened the front door and tiptoed outside, the keys in her hand and the afternoon sun high in the sky; it warmed her cheeks as she walked through the grass, taking the familiar route to the dirt track which sat to the north-east, not too far from Walker's place. She could hear the water flowing gently – the water she'd been swimming in only hours ago. Somewhere in the forest she could hear a woodpecker drumming away, accompanied by the shrill calls of a blackbird. She thought about the birds as she walked, her heart hammering in her chest. She wondered whether they felt it too, the tension that sat like a cloud over the places she had once found solace. It was suffocating.

She took one last look over her shoulder, then she started to run.

CHAPTER TWENTY-EIGHT

She could see Cal's truck in the distance, parked up in its usual spot. Ida felt her stomach jolt at the sight of it, her body remembering a time when his arrival would be something to celebrate. She quickly quashed the feeling and it was replaced almost immediately by a sadness that rung in her ears and gripped hold of her heart. It consumed her.

Cal's lies didn't just put an end to their relationship and the pretence of what he'd been trying to keep up; they put an end to Ida's way of life, to her simple way of living, sheltered from the burden of responsibility and expectations. She knew that sooner or later she would need to go back home – wherever that was now – and start over. She knew that there would be questions to answer and things to straighten out but she just couldn't bring herself to think about that right now. She wondered whether the real reason she hadn't confronted Cal yet was that she was trying to delay the inevitable end to everything she knew.

As she drew nearer to the truck she couldn't help but wonder how much Maeve's death had impacted how she'd handled the truth about Cal. Would she have been more inclined to rush home if she knew Maeve was there waiting for her? Would it have given her the incentive to walk right up to Cal and tell him she knew everything? To take the keys to his truck and drive off over the hills, leaving him here in the prison he'd created for her? She suspected the impact was immeasurable – it was a lot easier to stay hidden in the wilderness when there was no one looking for you; no one waiting for you on the other side. Her friends had long since stopped trying, her mother had died four years ago and her dad had never been part of her life. Violet and Ivy were the only family she had left, and they wouldn't remember her now. To them, it was as though she'd never even existed.

Ida glanced over towards the river and further north to where Walker's hut sat eclipsed by the landscape. She realised now that she'd been hoping to see him out walking Chief or continuing his swim in the river – she'd veered off in that direction without even realising it, led by her heart instead of her head. She corrected her course, turning away from the river and back towards the dirt path, to the rolling hills in the distance which had lost their air of mystery since her trip into Hamilton.

She used to think of them as her boundary; her limit. She could go no further than the hills because of the danger which lurked beyond – a danger which felt so palpable that she had never wandered anywhere near. A danger which had kept Walker hidden for so long. She wondered now how different the last three years of her life would have been if she would have known he was there, just miles away, with nothing but the land between them.

She kept looking back over her shoulder expecting Cal to come running towards her shouting her name, but as she reached the truck and made one final glance back towards the house she realised she'd made it without interruption. She pressed the button on the keys which unlocked the door and climbed into the driver's side. The truck was packed full of things which now repulsed her; she imagined Cal going to a supermarket and selecting all the bland foods with long shelf lives but little taste. She could imagine him grinning to himself as he reached the checkout, perhaps making a joke to the young woman at the till.

Cal always liked to flirt with other women in front of Ida. It made her feel uncomfortable and inferior in every way, but she'd told herself it was just his personality – or had Cal told her that? *I'm an extrovert, Ida, it's just how I am. Stop trying to change me.*

Ida recalled a birthday party they'd had at their house for Cal the year before they came here. She'd spent a long time arranging it, ensuring everything was just as Cal would like it – his favourite foods, his favourite beer, the house clean and tidy and decorated tastefully with birthday bunting and balloons. She'd only invited Cal's friends and their partners knowing that inviting her own friends or family would just cause arguments she didn't have the energy for – not that she had any friends or family left. Cal's family lived all over the country; she'd never actually met them and Cal had told her they weren't close, so it ended up just being ten of them – Cal, Ida, his four friends and their wives or girlfriends. She didn't particularly get on with any of them but she knew it would mean a lot to Cal.

The night went surprisingly well and by the end she'd almost lost the sense of panic and dread that had accompanied her for weeks at the thought of it; she hadn't been able to sleep and her neck and shoulders ached from the tension, but now that she saw everyone getting along and having a good time she began to feel herself relaxing.

Cal's oldest friend was Ethan and, if Ida had to pick, he was the one she would choose to speak to out of the group. He was tall and slim with a mop of curly brown hair – he worked in IT and was largely boring but unassuming, so Ida felt comfortable enough to be stood talking to him in the kitchen while everyone else chatted away happily in the dining room. Cal had walked in while they were having a conversation about the local restaurants in the area.

'Private party for two?' he'd asked. He laughed but it was hollow, a laugh Ida could tell was for Ethan's benefit rather than her own. His eyes narrowed as she busied herself tidying up the buffet she'd spent hours preparing.

'Just chatting about the new Thai restaurant that's opened,' Ethan said, his hands shoved in his pockets as he leant against the kitchen worktop.

'Better food there than Ida's cooking.' Cal looked at the spread on the table in front of Ida. 'I mean, she tries...'

Ida didn't speak and Ethan looked awkwardly between the two of them, Cal showing no sign of jesting.

'I'd better go and find Verity.' Ethan moved towards the door but before he got there Verity entered. She'd dressed up for the occasion in a way that seemed quite inappropriate to Ida in her jeans and blouse combo. Verity was wearing a strapless black dress with a deep plunge at the front and stiletto heels she'd refused to take off at the door. 'I was just coming to find you,' Ethan said, 'do you want a drink?'

'Yes, I'll have another Pimms,' she said, tossing her long blonde hair over her shoulder. Ethan quickly disappeared from the room, apparently delighted to have a reason to leave.

'You look amazing tonight, V.' Ida hated that Cal called her that – no one else did, it was like a private pet name that seemed a little too personal. 'That dress... very sexy. I bet Ethan can't wait to get you home.'

Ida stood wondering whether Cal realised she was still there. She wanted to scream; she wanted to shout about how inappropriate that dress was for a small gathering at someone's house; she wanted to say it wasn't sexy, it was slutty and not at all classy. But of course, she didn't, she just stood wishing the ground would open up beneath her.

Verity laughed, a high-pitched giggle that rung in Ida's ears long after she'd stopped. 'Oh, Callum, you're so naughty! I don't think Ethan has even noticed, you know what he's like.' She rolled her eyes and tucked her hair behind her ear, twirling a long piece around her finger.

Cal stepped closer to her. 'Well he ought to notice...' He kept his voice loud enough for Ida to hear but low enough that it would sound conspiratorial. 'Before someone else does!'

Verity giggled again, her hand grazing Cal's arm as she threw her head back elaborately. She never looked over at Ida, it was as though she didn't exist. Cal's own dismissal of Ida's feelings seemed to be rubbing off on his friends, an infectious ignorance which she wanted no part of. She'd heard enough, she felt humiliated, tears stinging her eyes. She stopped what she was doing and walked out of the kitchen, straight through the dining room where a couple of his friends sat sharing a cigar, and straight up to her bedroom. She closed the door and lay down on the bed, wondering how the hell she had ended up a shadow.

She began by looking through the compartments in the door but they yielded little in the way of evidence – a McDonald's burger wrapper which could be old although she knew it wasn't; an old map, tattered and worn; a couple of pens; a half-eaten packet of mints; a pair of sunglasses. Nothing of value to Ida.

She checked under the driver's seat then worked her way round to the passenger side, repeating the process of checking the door compartment and underneath the seat before turning her attention to the glovebox. It was so crammed full of things that papers spilled out as she opened it – old MOT certificates and garage receipts. Four of the documents were from the last three years – one showing work that had been done to the chassis and three itemising MOT repairs. Ida looked at the date and imagined the conversation with Cal in her head.

'*These receipts, they're recent,*' she would say, holding the papers out for him to see.

Cal would look at her with his head tilted to one side. '*Baby, we still need to repair vehicles, how else do you think we get around the country?*' He would work the conversation back to all the things he was doing for the country, his heroism and bravery, the fact that he never thought it was enough.

Ida put them to one side; they weren't enough. She carried on searching, occasionally checking out towards the house to ensure he was nowhere to be seen. She found a small first-aid kit and a bottle of de-icer, an ice scraper and a pair of headphones. Tucked at the back beneath the green first-aid kit she came across his wallet and, beside it, his mobile phone.

She turned it over in her hands, looking at it as though it was a relic from a time she could barely recall. It wasn't too dissimilar to the one she remembered having when they came here – slim and black with a large touchscreen. She pressed the button on the side and it came on, lighting up the screen and asking for a passcode or fingerprint. Ida stared at it, willing it to work; when it didn't she had a guess at the passcode using the one she knew he'd used before – his birthday. Incorrect. She wanted to try again but she had no idea where to start and the last thing she wanted to do was block the phone – she wasn't sure how many attempts she would get. Instead, she turned the phone off and searched through the wallet.

It was brown and leather and contained only cash, no credit or debit cards. Ida frowned – it was what she'd been banking on, she realised, credit cards with a recent issue date. Cal had specifically told her that no banks were operating anymore – money had become irrelevant so banks had ceased to exist – so she had hoped that proof to the contrary would be enough for her, that they would give her the confidence to believe in herself and question him the way she wanted to. She wanted answers, but she wouldn't get them without evidence that not even Cal could twist or distort; something personal, something that would refute the copious lies he'd told about his own life. What had he been doing while Ida was hidden away? Where had he been going? And who with? The book felt too far removed, too vague. She could hear him in her mind telling her that certain books were still published or that it was a simple misprint. She needed something solid, something to hold on to and focus on.

She counted the cash – almost two hundred pounds – then put it neatly back inside the wallet, wondering what his excuse would be for having so much money on him when it was no longer required. She thought it would make her feel good to take it and burn it, to tell him it was a symbolic gesture, cutting off the thing that had once controlled them – she could watch Cal's face change as he watched it burn, unable to do a single thing about it. But afterwards, she would still be in the same position and so would he, albeit two hundred pounds worse off. She wedged the wallet back under the first-aid kit and shut the glovebox, the phone still in her hand. If she could just find a way to open it, to place the little sensor under his thumb, then she would have access to things she couldn't even imagine.

'Ida!'

She turned quickly, her neck cricking with the sudden harshness of the movement. Cal was coming, running through the long grass with a look of horror on his face. How had he got so close without her realising? She quickly slipped the phone into her shorts pocket and grabbed the can of petrol and bag of food she'd placed ready by the door.

'Ida, what are you doing?' Cal reached her with a thin layer of sweat glistening on his forehead.

'I didn't want to wake you. I thought I'd make a start.'

'You should have waited for me.' His tone was short and heated but, realising his anger didn't equate to the situation, he quickly tried to make the shift to caring fiancé, his eyes softening along with his voice. 'I don't want you tiring yourself out, you've been through enough.'

'I'm fine.' Ida shrugged. She began walking back towards the house with the supplies in her hands and the weight of the phone in her pocket; she hoped he couldn't see it bulging through the material of her shorts. To her, it felt like the most obvious thing in the world. A huge secret, too big to hide and impossible to ignore.

CHAPTER TWENTY-NINE

Cal hauled two cans of petrol out of the boot then shouted to Ida, asking her to lock the truck. She put down the supplies and reached into her pocket for the keys; she'd forgot she had them, her mind set on the phone and the secrets it might contain. She pressed the button to lock up then dropped the keys back into her pocket. Cal quickly caught up with her, almost jogging to make up the distance between them.

'Ida, what's wrong?'

'Nothing's wrong. I'm just tired.' She kept her eyes ahead, not turning to look at Cal. She couldn't see anything but how wrong she'd been when she looked at him, and everything that had happened as a result.

'That's why we went for a lie down, so you could sleep.'

Ida could hear the uncertainty in his voice; he wasn't used to her being the less loving one. It was new territory for them both and Ida could tell that Cal wasn't sure how to act. The years they'd spent living this way had blurred what came before, the relationship they'd had and the roles they'd assumed.

'I just couldn't sleep. Maybe I'm overtired, I don't know.'

'Let me take care of you, baby.' His tone was pleading and it turned Ida's stomach, knowing how false it was. He didn't want to take care of her, he wanted to control her, to keep her tucked up in bed where he could see her.

'How long will you be here for?' she asked. She realised she was holding her breath, waiting for an answer she wasn't sure she'd like.

'A few days,' he said. 'We're really busy back at the base at the minute, the warmer weather has caused a spike in cases.' He sighed heavily as though the emotional exhaustion of it all was taking its toll. Ida knew he was waiting for her to comment on his dedication, to make some remark about how selfless he was being or how awful it must be for him, but she just couldn't bring herself to say the things he needed to hear. They walked on in silence, Ida watching her feet cut through the grass, spotting the wildflowers which stood out among the green, letting her mind drift to the quiet beauty of the land. After a while, Cal broke the silence. 'I've brought something for you.'

The usual excitement at hearing these words didn't arrive. Instead, a bitter resentment simmered in her chest, compressing her heart and causing a lump in her throat. She couldn't help but think about all the times he had said this – all the times he had arrived with something which seemed like a wonderful gesture but was actually a last-minute purchase at a supermarket – the wine, the chocolates, the Southern Comfort. Even the coffee, which had seemed so thoughtful only weeks ago, now seemed particularly cruel. Had he emptied half of the contents out before giving it to her? Or had he brought it along from home, half used?

A year after they'd moved here, he'd told her he'd brought something particularly special with him but she had to wait until sunset. She'd been giddy with excitement, watching the sun go down and waiting for the big reveal. They'd walked out into the fields hand in hand and he'd got down on one knee, the setting sun and deep pink sky the perfect backdrop.

'I know it won't be the wedding we'd dreamed of. I know it won't be legal or traditional or fancy, but I don't care about any of that stuff. I only care about *us*. This past year has been one of the happiest of my life. I know how crazy that sounds, but it's true. Just me and you with no interruptions; it's been nothing short of perfect. I want us to make a promise to each other: someday, somehow, we *will* be husband and wife.' He'd pulled a little blue box out of his pocket and opened it. A diamond and sapphire ring sat in the middle of a velvet cushion, a white gold band glistening in the fading sunlight. Ida's hands covered her mouth, catching the scream she wanted to let out. 'Ida, will you marry me?'

She'd cried happy tears and sunk to her knees as Cal slipped the ring on her finger. She'd thrown her arms around his neck and they'd made love in the grassland, jubilant and full of hope for the future. It was as though the old Cal had stayed behind, the controlling, angry man who'd begun to chip away at her happiness now nothing but a dwindling memory. With that ring on her finger she could barely remember him that way; she could barely recall what they used to argue about or who they'd been before. This was the man she'd fallen in love with, the man who'd swept her off her feet and saved her from the horrors he had to continue to experience. For her.

He was her hero.

———

Back in the house, Cal held out his hand to her. 'Keys?' She took them out of her pocket and handed them to him. 'Wait there, let me find your present.' He rummaged around inside his bag and pulled out a plastic Tupperware box. He opened the lid to reveal a chocolate cake. 'I persuaded one of the cooks at the military base to make this for you. Traded some of my rations for it.' He smiled, a big toothy smile that carried expectations. He needed her to be grateful – giddy, even. He needed boundless appreciation and excitement. He wanted what Ida felt unable to give, she just didn't have the energy. Instead, she stood blinking away the tears that were gathering, tears of anger and frustration, sadness and loss. She wanted to talk to Maeve, she wanted to apologise to her for being blind to the reality she'd tried so desperately to make her see.

'What... what's wrong? Ida?' He put the lid back on the box and placed it down heavily on top of the table. He stood looking at her, unsure whether to comfort her or admonish her.

'I'm sorry,' she found herself saying. 'I'm sorry, I'm just... I'm overwhelmed.' She could hear how pathetic she sounded and she knew how touched he would be that his offering had reduced her to tears. She hated herself for it. She clasped her hands together and spun her engagement ring round on her finger. She'd wanted to take it off and she'd had to restrain herself on more than one occasion from throwing it into the river, but she knew he would notice if it was missing. It no longer felt like it belonged on her hand – it felt too big and awkward and she'd found herself fidgeting with it endlessly.

'Oh, baby!' His smile was back and his hands were pulling her into him. 'Come here, silly.'

'I think I need to get some sleep,' she said, burying her face into his chest so she didn't have to look at him.

He kissed her on top of her head and stroked her hair. 'I think that's a good idea. Go and get some sleep and I'll put all this away.'

She nodded, not daring to look up at him. 'Okay.'

'I'll make us a nice meal tonight and we can have a proper catch-up.' He took hold of her hands in his and smiled. 'I've missed you.' He looked so sincere that she almost fell for it. He pulled her towards him and kissed her on the lips, his hands moving up to her face and holding her there, suspended in a moment she couldn't wait to break free from. 'Go and get some rest.'

She nodded and smiled weakly as she turned, walking off towards the bedroom and hoping that this time he wouldn't follow. Once inside she closed the door and took the phone out of her pocket. She couldn't wait to be free of it, it felt as though it was burning a hole in her leg and she'd kept expecting it to go off despite knowing it wasn't possible. She looked around the room wondering where to hide it, then opted for under the mattress, on her side of the bed. It would be easy to access in the night there, when Cal was in a deep sleep and oblivious. She pressed the mattress down firmly on top of it then lay in the bed, pulling a sheet over her. She was drained but sleep did not come easily; she was plagued by images of Maeve telling her it was too late, her words mingling with the blood that dripped from her mouth.

CHAPTER THIRTY

Ida woke under a fog of confusion. She hadn't meant to fall asleep, she'd fought it long into the night, trying to keep her eyes open and her mind clear, but eventually exhaustion had caught up with her.

They'd shared a meal of chilli and rice together followed by a slice of the chocolate cake he'd bought. The sponge tasted dry and the frosting too sweet. The conversation had felt forced but Cal hadn't seemed to notice; she'd nodded in all the right places and her cheeks burned from the false smile she'd held there. After they'd gone to bed, she'd rolled over and faced the wall, horrified at the thought of Cal trying to undress her, to kiss her when she didn't want to be kissed. To Ida's relief, he hadn't protested.

Cal was in the kind of deep sleep that made his eyes flicker and his breathing rapid and shallow. Ida wondered if he was dreaming and, if so, what about. Her? His lies? She wished she could delve into his mind and sort through what was in there. She lay on her side watching him, noticing all the things she'd failed to see in recent years.

His beard was a little too neat, his eyebrows too trimmed

and his hair too styled and preened. His appearance had the air of someone trying too hard to look rugged and wild, but maybe she was only able to see it now she had the comparison of Walker, whose hair seemed to grow from every available space, in every available direction. And it wasn't just Cal's hair – he *smelled* clean, too, and his clothes looked fresh and washed, absent of the holes and the threads which permeated Walker's.

As she lay comparing the only two men she knew, she let Cal slip deeper into the realms of sleep, breathing as quietly as she could and lying as still as possible. She traced her fingertip down his forearm, through the wiry hairs and onto the back of his hand, testing the boundaries of his sleep. Cal didn't move or respond, but still she waited, just to be sure.

Her thoughts drifted to the first night they'd spent together in Ida's flat. They'd been out for a meal and then to the cinema in town. When they arrived back at Ida's place Cal suggested they open a bottle of wine. They'd met a couple of months before at the local gym, Cal was the instructor for a class she'd signed up for and Ida had been flattered by his attention; there were so many other women in the class who'd flirted shamelessly with him, but he only seemed to have eyes for Ida.

They'd enjoyed several dates under the guise of personal training sessions before progressing to a walk along the canal and a coffee at a nearby café. Soon after, the pretence slipped away and they were seeing each other almost every night – the beginning of a relationship Ida hadn't even realised she was open to. Ida had never invited him to stay over before; there was something about him that made her a little uneasy at first but she couldn't put her finger on what it was. Maybe it was the way he looked at her; sometimes his stare was so intense that it made her feel... *intimidated*. As though he was looking right into her soul.

Eventually she'd let her guard fade away; time had brought

familiarity and she'd begun to feel at ease in his company. She tried to distinguish between having genuine feelings and simply enjoying the compliment of having a man like Cal pursue her, but it was difficult to separate the two. His persistence had interfered with her ability to think straight and eventually led to them spending the night together. She'd woke the following morning to him next to her in bed.

'Morning, beautiful.' He'd kissed her head and stroked her hair, he'd been attentive to her every need and made her feel like the only woman in the world. The doubt naturally began to disappear, replaced instead by a happiness she'd never experienced before. It was as though she'd had her eyes closed her whole life, and now she was finally seeing the beauty in everything. She fell in love; hard and fast.

Ida sat up and waited, watching Cal for any sign of disturbance. When she was satisfied he was still sleeping she slipped out from under the sheet and quietly knelt down beside the bed, her hand moving under the mattress and her fingers grasping for the slim shape of the phone. When she found it she pulled it out slowly, careful not to make any sudden movement in her haste to unlock it. She put it under her pillow first, lying back down in bed and listening for the reassuring sound of Cal's breathing.

After a few minutes she decided it was now or never, she didn't have endless nights like this to take her time and pluck up her courage; she had to do it now. She took the phone from under her pillow, turned it on and positioned it as close to Cal's hand as she could. Then she moved his thumb over the sensor and held her breath. The backlight flickered, changing from plain white to a photograph. It had worked. She'd unlocked it. Endless information was now at her fingertips.

She had to work hard to keep herself quiet, her heart was pounding in her chest and her breathing was erratic. She realised she hadn't planned this far ahead, she hadn't allowed herself to think about what she would do if it worked. She lay for a moment, the phone clutched in her hands, panicking. She decided the best thing to do would be to get away from Cal; she wanted to be able to look through the contents without him lying next to her, the threat of him waking interfering with her ability to process anything.

Quietly, she walked out of the bedroom and closed the door behind her. She headed straight for the door to the outside, her bare feet tapping quietly against the floorboards. She reasoned that if Cal found her out there she would be able to discard the phone somewhere temporarily and tell him that she'd needed some air, that she couldn't sleep or that she had a headache. She crept out into the dark, the cool night air prickling her skin and the hazy light of the moon guiding her out into the fields. She hadn't thought to bring a coat or her robe but she found that she didn't mind, the cold stimulated her and helped to clear her head. When she was a hundred metres or so from the house, barely able to see the ground beneath her, she sat down and took out the phone, hoping the long grass would create a barrier and disguise the glow from the display.

She hadn't processed the photograph on the screen while she was in the bedroom, the apps which littered it and the panic which blurred her focus had prevented her from taking it in. But now that she was alone she saw it quite clearly: it was a picture of a little boy with a toothy grin and curly blond hair. He was wearing a white shirt and a pale-blue bow tie, his cheeks rosy and pink. Cute, Ida thought, but why had Cal got this as his background? It made no sense.

Ida stared at it for a while, into the grey-blue eyes she seemed to recognise, not wanting to acknowledge what she could see so clearly. She clicked on the gallery icon and scrolled through the photos – hundreds if not thousands of them. The most recent were of the same boy with the same grey-blue eyes as Cal's. There was a photo of the two of them together, the resemblance striking. Then, further down, a photo of them both with a woman. She knew that woman – she recognised the long blonde hair and the straight, narrow nose.

It was Verity.

Ida sat scrolling through the photos for a long time, swiping through the endless pictures of what looked to be a perfect family. Last August, there'd been photos of them on holiday, the little boy on the beach and Verity in a black triangle bikini, a cocktail in her hand. The pictures dated right back to two years ago when a baby dominated the photos – a newborn cradled against Cal's bare chest; a family portrait of Cal and Verity looking adoringly at their son; the little boy wrapped in a blanket with a teddy bear beside him declaring his name. Otto.

A year later, photos of a wedding at a grand building Ida recognised but couldn't recall the name of, a stately house with an impressive fountain outside. Verity had worn a strapless fishtail gown with a floor-length veil, a pink-and-white cascading bouquet clutched in her hands. Cal had looked smart in a three-piece suit, navy-blue tweed with a gold tie. Otto was dressed like a mini version of his dad, stealing the show with his beaming smile.

Despite the anger she felt towards Cal, despite everything he'd put her through, her heart ached with an illogical yet burning jealousy. They looked happy, and Ida had not been expecting to find something which would make her feel this way. It was as though she was looking at the life she should have had, the wedding she should have planned with Cal and the dress she should have chosen with Maeve, the baby she should have held against her chest, the love she should have felt for him.

She spent so long looking through the photos that she almost forgot to do anything else. She could see the crimson hues of the sun on the horizon, the day hinting at its arrival. Ida wished she could pause time, to exist in this moment without the pressure of the impending morning. She clicked back to the main screen and decided to look through his messages. There was no signal where she was, no option to call anyone or search for anything that wasn't already available, but she could read the messages he'd already received. The last was from Verity.

> We'll miss you! Have a good trip. V x

Ida scrolled through, reading what appeared to be normal conversations between an ordinary couple – requests to pick up shopping, photos of Otto, messages about what time they'd be home or what they wanted for dinner. Cal still worked as a personal trainer, Ida discovered, but he now owned his own business – she'd found a screenshot Cal had sent to Verity of an advertisement in the local paper.

It wasn't until she scrolled back to March when she found the first signs that all was not as rosy as it seemed. Cal had texted Verity telling her he needed to go away for a few days for a training course. Ida had looked at the date – it would have been when he last visited her in Wales.

Verity had responded:

> Are we going to talk about last night?

Cal hadn't replied so Verity had sent him another text:

> Callum? You hurt me. Again. This can't keep happening.

Ida had read and reread that message many times, remembering years ago when she had sent messages just like this, when they were still under the pretence that Cal's temper was an exception rather than the norm.

Cal had responded:

> You shouldn't have spoken to me that way, you know how tired I am from work. Everything I do is for you and Otto, and you never appreciate any of it.

Ida had an unexpected pang of sympathy for Verity as she read her reply:

> I'm sorry. I do appreciate you, you're a great husband and a wonderful father.

There were several other exchanges like this, one just after Christmas and one following their holiday in August. Verity's reactions had started off angry; once she'd even left him and moved in with her parents. Cal had begged her for forgiveness and told her it would never happen again, that Otto deserved to have his family together. As time went on, his apologies fell away along with her expectations of anything more. It was like watching her own life playing back to her, acted out by someone else.

The sunlight seeped into the sky as Ida's eyes became dry and gritty. She tried to blink away the fatigue but the emotional toll of the information she'd found only exacerbated it. She kept stealing glances back to the house, checking Cal wasn't stood watching her or heading her way, a confused look in his eyes as she sat encircled by the grass. She scrolled through other messages from friends and clients, a few flirty exchanges with someone he was helping to train for a marathon and an exchange with his friend Olly about a stag party he owed money for in July – they were going to Ibiza for Henry's stag and, further down the chain of messages, Olly had mentioned Ethan.

Ethan is coming.

Are you asking or telling?

Telling.

The next messages were to do with the itinerary and what was owed and Cal hadn't replied. Ida had met Olly, Henry and Ethan several times. Cal had been friends with them since university and Ida knew his relationship with Verity would have caused upset within the group – it had to have. Cal wouldn't like the fact that Ethan wasn't cast out to make his life more comfortable.

'Ida?' She whipped her head round to see Cal stood at the front of the house looking for her, a hoody pulled up over his head and his hands on his hips.

Ida turned off the phone and looked around; there was a yellow gorse to her right with thick shrubbery around the base. She placed the phone at its roots and made sure it was well covered, then she stood up and forced a smile onto her face, waving at Cal.

'What are you doing?'

'I couldn't sleep.' She crossed her arms over her body, realising now how cold she was. She began walking back to the house, stealing one last look at where she'd put the phone, ensuring it was hidden.

'What were you doing sitting out in the field?' He noticed

Ida shivering and stepped towards her, his warm hands feeling her bare arms. 'You're bloody freezing, Ida. What's going on with you?'

'Nothing, I just couldn't sleep. I went for a walk round and decided to sit and watch the sunrise.'

Cal frowned, his eyes narrowing suspiciously. 'Is there something going on? You've been acting strange since I got here. Really distant and, to be honest, quite rude.'

Ida took a deep breath, stalling. Since Cal had arrived here she'd felt conflicted, stuck in a constant battle between wanting to shout the truth from the top of the hills and wanting to bury it deep underground. She wanted him to know that she knew everything, yet she couldn't bring herself to admit it; she'd wanted to find evidence, but now that she had it she didn't know how to present it; she wanted to understand why, yet she hadn't been prepared for the truth to sting so much; she was angry but scared; furious yet sad.

Cal stood looking at her, watching with his steely eyes, waiting for an answer she couldn't give. And all the while, with her mind in turmoil, her heart was telling her to run north towards the hills.

Towards Walker.

CHAPTER THIRTY-ONE

I da managed to placate Cal by making herself seem like the vulnerable shell of a woman she'd been when he brought her here, the woman who questioned herself more than she would ever question others. The woman whose internal voice had become cruel and unforgiving, goading herself relentlessly. It took Ida a long time to realise that she would never dream of speaking to others the way that she spoke to herself. The wilderness had helped her to understand herself better than she had in a long time; it was as though a fog had lifted, allowing her to challenge her inner thoughts and the negative cycle she'd become lost in. It had given her the space and the time to descend into the quiet and find a peace she hadn't had for as long as she could remember. Her kindness came back, and she began to like herself again.

Ida could see Cal's eyes soften as she allowed the tears to fall. 'I'm struggling, Cal. I'm struggling without you.' It pained her to say it; it seemed like an echo from three years before, when she would plead with him to stay with her, to take care of her. 'I feel so alone all the time,' she cried, wiping away the tears that were for something else entirely.

'Baby, I'm here.' Cal pulled her towards him, shushing her as he wrapped his arms around her and stroked her hair, her cheek pressed to his chest. She wondered whether he held his son this way when he was upset, whether he shushed him too. Ida couldn't help her imagination running wild, asking herself the questions she was unable to answer: was he a good dad? Was he hands-on? When did his relationship with Verity begin? Were they having an affair while Ida was still with him in Surrey? Had Verity moved into the home they'd once shared? Did he love them both? Or neither of them?

'We have to make the most of the time we have together. Come on, I'll make us some breakfast.' He held her hand and guided her back into the house, Ida's skin still cold to the touch. 'Here.' He handed her the blanket from the sofa and she sat down as he began busying himself in the kitchen. 'I brought eggs,' he said, smiling. 'The chickens are doing well, we've got quite a few at the camp now. I should be able to start coming here more often. I can bring fresh produce and eggs and the materials for the roof...'

'More often?'

Cal looked over at her from the kitchen and paused what he was doing for a moment. 'I've been thinking,' he said. 'I should be here with you more.'

'But... but what about your job?'

Cal shrugged then cracked some eggs over a pan. 'I've given the last three years of my life to helping people. I don't want it to come at a cost. I don't want to neglect you.'

Ida's heart pounded – the words she would have been overjoyed to hear only weeks ago now hitting her with a force she hadn't been prepared for. 'You're not neglecting me. I'm okay, really, it's just been a difficult few weeks.' She cleared her throat and when she spoke again she tried to sound stronger; more capable. 'I know how important your work is. I know how needed you are. I wouldn't want to be selfish and take you away from that.' She was treading a fine line, she realised, between sounding as though she was being understanding and selfless and sounding as though she didn't want him there.

'You haven't been selfish, that's my point. And now look at you. You need help, baby. I need to come back more, and I will.'

Ida turned away from Cal and looked into the empty fireplace taking a long, steadying breath. She was trying to work out how he would manage to explain it to Verity; frequent trips to Wales without mobile network coverage weren't a usual occurrence for most couples, but then Ida remembered how persuasive Cal could be.

'Here you go.' He handed her a plate with two fried eggs and some chopped tomatoes. She looked over to see that once again he'd forgone the eggs himself, sitting down next to her with a plate of the tomatoes and a couple of crackers. She wondered whether it was pre-planned; a purposeful effort to make him seem like the gallant hero he was trying to portray, sacrificing his own needs so that Ida would have more.

Cal had always been meticulous about his nutrition, keeping food diaries and counting his calories and protein. It came hand in hand with his job, he said. Ida had always thought it seemed like a little more than that, though; to her, it had felt like just another part of his life he liked absolute control over. If he had a drink or a dessert when they were out, the next day he would eat cleaner and train harder. As she watched him now, slurping the tomato juice off of the spoon, traces of red getting caught in his beard, she wondered whether he saw coming out here as a way to get back on track, to cut out the temptations and hit the reset button – a health retreat or something similar.

Ida picked at her food, eating just enough to stave off Cal's comments and concerns. She felt nauseous and her breathing was shallow, as though she couldn't catch a full breath of air. Cal took the plates into the kitchen.

'You need me to do anything?' he asked. Ida shook her head. 'I'll come back with some materials for the roof. Don't worry, I'll make sure I'm back before the temperature drops. It should hold until then.'

'Okay.'

Cal sat back down next to her and tucked her hair behind her ear. 'It must have been scary,' he said.

'What must have?'

'The storm.'

'Oh. Yes, it was.' She could tell he wanted her to elaborate, to fill him with tales of how petrified she'd been, of how she'd wished that he was there to protect her, but she refused to fuel his ego.

'I'll go and get some firewood – get you stocked up.' He kissed her on the cheek. 'Why don't you get some sleep?'

Ida nodded and pulled the blanket tighter around her shoulders. 'I think I will,' she said.

She waited for Cal to leave then stood by the kitchen sink looking out of the window, watching as he edged closer to the river, disappearing below the hill for a moment then rising quickly up the other side, the axe in his hand. He soon vanished into the dense woodland, leaving Ida stood there full of uncertainty. She was worried that she'd left it too long, that old emotions and routine had started to make way for doubts, to make her question whether it was worth the upset and disruption. She didn't want it to be about the moment – those few seconds where she would get to feel some kind of satisfaction when she told him she knew everything. It had to be about more than that; it had to be about wanting something more for herself and not about simply wanting less for Cal.

She had her proof. She had irrefutable evidence that Cal

had been leading an ordinary life while she'd been stuck here, contained by walls he'd built. And now what? What was she waiting for? Cal wasn't going to bring it up, it was down to her and her only, and yet there was something stopping her. When she thought about what would come after the moment of truth, she was filled with dread. It wasn't just about Cal's reaction – although she wasn't looking forward to that – it was everything else. What would she do? Where would she go? She'd become so used to living out here, living this way, not governed by other people's time or society's expectations. She wasn't sure how she would slip back into life beyond the hills.

She'd been a teacher once, a long time ago, at a little primary school in the suburbs. She'd loved teaching and being around children; their positivity and laughter made her feel lighter. She'd been part of a small team that were like a second family to her and the headteacher was someone she respected greatly – Simon Gables, a man whose passion and enthusiasm was infectious.

The first time Ida had introduced Cal to everyone was at the staff Christmas party. Simon had sung Ida's praises and told Cal how she would make a fine headteacher herself one day. Simon was almost fifty; happily married with two grown-up children. A father figure to Ida in many ways. But Cal didn't see it that way; his jealousy lingered long after the last drinks had been drunk and the goodbyes had been said. That Easter, she'd handed in her notice. She'd lied and told Simon that she planned to travel and he'd smiled and said all the things she needed to hear. But there was a trace of doubt in his tone and in the way that he'd looked at her. He told her she would always have a job to go back to and a friend to confide in, should she need it. Ida had cried all the way home, and for a long time after. She'd left a piece of herself at that school, but by then she'd grown used to leaving pieces of herself behind, never quite feeling whole.

Before she could question herself or her reasons, she threw the blanket onto the sofa and pulled on a pair of shorts and a T-shirt. Then she slipped on her shoes, flinging open the door and closing it behind her. She didn't have much time.

CHAPTER THIRTY-TWO

Ida ran across the fields, her lungs stinging and her throat dry as she propelled herself forwards, one foot in front of the other, allowing her steps to account for a decision she hadn't realised she'd made. She ran as fast as she could, the ground uneven and the tall grass whipping at her bare legs as she cut through it. The sun was hanging to the east, another cloudless day, the heat swelling around her as she moved. She ran past the dirt track and followed the river round to the cluster of trees where, tucked behind them, Walker's hut stood small and squat. She stopped abruptly, catching her breath.

She could hear music – Simon and Garfunkel's 'The Sound of Silence' playing over the noise of the water flowing to her left. She stood and listened, taking a moment to herself to try to gather the thoughts she could not control. When the song faded away she took it as her cue, walking round to the front of the hut to find Walker outside with Chief. He was grilling something over the fire, a beer in his hand. He didn't look surprised to see her, he simply held up a bottle and raised his eyebrows, asking her in his own way if she would like to join him.

'No, thank you,' she said.

He shrugged and put it back down, returning his attention to the fire.

'I need to talk to you.' She didn't know what to do with herself, conscious all of a sudden about the way she was standing and how she held herself. She didn't want to seem confrontational but she was also aware that was exactly what she was doing... confronting him.

'Okay.' He turned to face her but only for a second, quickly turning back to the fire, prodding at the meat as the orange flames danced among the coal. Ida wanted to grab hold of him and make him stop; to force him to look at her and let her know that she was being listened to. It frustrated her, the way he always seemed slightly out of her reach.

'Cal's here,' she said.

'I know.' There was no malice or judgement in his tone, just a simple acknowledgement that he was aware. Ida wasn't sure what she expected – did she want him to be angry? Jealous? She didn't know, but she wanted something more than a one-way conversation with the occasional grunted response.

'I found his phone. He has a wife. And a son.' It felt more real now that she'd said it aloud, giving the information she already knew a life of its own and watching as it landed with Walker. He looked at her for a moment, a flicker of shock in his eyes. 'Aren't you going to say anything?' she asked, taking a step closer towards him. She needed to keep some distance between them – some physical space for them both to breathe to account for the emotional gap she was trying to close.

'What do you want me to say? It's not my place to tell you what to do.'

'I don't want you to tell me what to do. I...'

Walker interjected. 'Then what do you want?' He threw out his arms as though already exasperated by the conversation. It made Ida want to cry. Was he right? Had she wanted him to tell her what to do? She was angry at herself as she realised that was probably true, to some extent; years of being told what to do by Cal had taken their toll and now she found herself seemingly unable to make a decision without the help of a man. 'It has to come from *you*.' He looked right at her now so as there was no doubt about what he was trying to convey.

Ida felt embarrassed for coming here, for looking to someone she barely knew to provide her with answers. But then she remembered everything they'd experienced together – he'd saved her life on more than one occasion; he'd held her as she sobbed and given her space to grieve. Hadn't they been through enough together to warrant a conversation when she needed it?

'I thought we were friends or... or... something. What am I supposed to do with all the things inside my head? I can't think straight, I've got no one!'

Neither of them spoke for a while. Walker took whatever it was he'd been cooking off of the fire and dropped it into Chief's bowl, then he sat down on one of the chairs and took a long drink of his beer.

'Forget all the things in your head,' he said. 'You *know* what you've got to do. You know it in your heart.'

Ida looked at him, her eyes narrowing. 'Is that some shitty advice you dish out when you can't be bothered to talk? *Listen to you heart?* That's bullshit! My *heart* is the reason I'm here!'

Walker didn't respond and in his silence all the questions and the doubts she'd buried over the previous weeks they'd shared together found new life, a momentum she couldn't stall.

'My name is Ida,' she shouted, catching herself by surprise. 'I was a teacher. A sister. An aunt. I lived in Surrey. I went to Pilates and out for cocktails with my friends. I watched Netflix and ordered take out. I played with my nieces and plaited their hair. I had a *life*.' Walker looked away as though the information was painful to hear, his head hung low, his eyes on the floor beneath him. 'Why don't you care? We spent all that time together and I...' She ran her fingers through her hair, pushing it away from her face. Her fingertips felt the coarse glue which still clung around her roots, the glue that Walker had used to fix the wound on her scalp. 'Why did you save me? Why did you let me stay here? Was it all for Maeve? To alleviate your guilt?' Walker shook his head, his eyes still on the ground. 'Why can't you *look* at me?' Her voice was louder now, commanding. Slowly, he looked up, his eyes meeting hers, but still he didn't speak. 'I want to know your name. I want to know why you're here and where you were before.'

'I can't be the reason you choose to stay.' His voice was low, barely above a whisper. It infuriated Ida that the few words he managed to say to her were devoid of any feelings or emotion. It made her feel worthless.

'After everything...' Ida began to cry. She didn't want to, but she couldn't help it. As the tears ran down her cheeks she wiped them away, angry at them for putting her on display like this, vulnerable and breaking – or perhaps already broken.

'Please don't cry.' Walker stood up and moved slowly towards her until he was standing close enough that he could reach out and touch her. But he didn't. 'I wish I could give you what you're looking for.'

'All I'm looking for is for someone to be honest with me.'

Walker sighed, turning back towards the house as though contemplating running away for a moment, but he didn't; he stayed. He turned back to her with his eyes full of the emotion he never usually let her see. It made Ida's heart ache.

'Have you ever asked yourself why I would choose to live out here like this?' he asked.

'Every day since I met you.'

'I wasn't always this way. I had a family once. A life.'

Ida had suspected he'd lost someone close to him; it seemed

to her to be the only explanation. Sometimes he wore the scars of loss so clearly that she could almost read them, but it was still difficult to hear him say it. She realised she'd been hoping she was wrong; she'd been hoping that somehow he'd been spared the hurt she'd assigned him in her imagination.

'What happened?' she asked, but she immediately regretted it; she didn't want to push him too hard. She felt as though they were on the brink of a conversation he hadn't had before, one that he'd spent a long time avoiding, and she was acutely aware of the sensitivity it required. She didn't want to let him down or say too much or not enough. It felt like a balancing act, delicate and fragile.

'We lost a child, and...' His voice caught in his throat, breaking under the weight of his emotions. He ran a hand over his face, a temporary mask while he gathered himself. 'I wasn't there for my wife. I couldn't be the man she needed me to be and I... I lost her too.'

Ida knew not to press him any further, to dig for more information that would only cause him pain. He'd revealed a part of himself he'd wanted to remain hidden and she knew that it would come at a considerable personal cost. She didn't know what to say, so she chose not to say anything at all. She reached out her hand and placed it on his chest, feeling the steady rhythm of his heart beating.

Walker put his hand on top of Ida's and gripped it tight. 'I can't do that again. I can't lose anyone else.'

Ida nodded – she understood completely.

CHAPTER THIRTY-THREE

Ida's chest felt tight, as though the air was being slowly compressed inside her lungs. She was conscious of the time. She knew she'd already been gone too long. Cal would probably be back at the house now, wondering where she'd gone. He would come looking for her, and she knew it would only be a matter of time before he'd find her.

She didn't want to leave, but she knew she couldn't stay here with Walker. There was something different in the air between them, the peace which once rested there now alive with possibilities that they both knew would not be straightforward.

'I have to go.' She let her hand fall from his chest. He didn't protest or try to hold her back, he simply nodded, acknowledging what he knew she needed to do.

She didn't say goodbye, she couldn't formulate the words in her mind which had already begun to panic, imagining Cal wandering around the fields looking for her. She took off, breaking into a run and heading south towards the house. She tired easily, the fatigue from the night before catching up with her and the heat from the sun slowing her down. Halfway back, when she felt enough distance had stretched out between her and Walker, she stopped and caught her breath. She could see the house from here, but she couldn't see Cal. She took long strides through the grass, her eyes frantically searching for any sign of him.

When she was a few hundred metres from the house, she saw him emerge from the front door. He looked around, spotting Ida walking briskly towards him. He didn't walk to meet her, he simply stood waiting for her with his hands on his hips. When she reached him he raised his eyebrows. 'Let me guess, you couldn't sleep?'

'I'm all out of sync. I'm so tired but I just can't seem to drift off.'

'So you decided to go for a walk?'

Ida couldn't read him. His tone wasn't angry but it wasn't particularly kind either; his stance wasn't threatening but nor was it welcoming.

'I thought some fresh air might help.'

'And did it?'

'Maybe a little. Shall I make us a drink?' Ida gestured towards the door but Cal was blocking it and he didn't move, he just stood watching her, searching her eyes. She used to hate it when he did this, whenever they argued over something she wasn't sure she'd done. He would glare at her, deep into her soul, and she would always wonder what it was he found there that seemed to repulse him.

'You haven't drank the coffee I brought you.'

'I was saving it.'

'For?'

Ida shrugged, trying to seem nonchalant, but it felt unnatural and she saw in Cal's eyes that he noticed it too. 'I just didn't want to use it all in case you couldn't get any more.'

'You haven't eaten much of the food either. It's almost like you haven't been here.'

Ida felt herself tense up, her shoulders hunching and her jaw tightening. He was goading her; Ida could tell that he knew something was wrong. She should be used to it by now – being treated this way – but the three years of relative peace had blinded her to what he was capable of.

Her mind drifted back to years before, when Ida's life had begun to change. It had happened slowly at first – his behaviour often misinterpreted by Ida as excessive care and concern. Soon, she realised she had made the switch between lying to Cal when she wanted to see her friends to just not seeing them at all – it was easier that way. She put his demands ahead of her own needs in every way, but she drew the line at her sister. She needed her. She needed *someone*. A knot had begun to unfurl in her stomach, painful and ever-present, and she wasn't sure it would ever go.

She'd met her sister after work, in a coffee shop close to the school. Maeve had worn her worry on her face, hugging Ida so tight she felt she might never let go.

'We're worried about you, Ida. You don't see anyone anymore, you don't return our calls or texts. What's going on? Is it Cal?'

They sat down at a little table overlooking a car park across the road. They ordered coffees and Ida did her best to steer the conversation away from Cal and towards work, the only thing she had to talk about that didn't involve the relationship Maeve so vehemently disapproved of.

'Ida, we need to talk about Cal. This isn't right. Look at you! You've lost weight, you look unwell.'

'I've lost weight because my boyfriend is a personal trainer!' Ida tried to make light of the situation, forcing a laugh she didn't mean. She *had* lost weight, unintentionally as well, but Cal had commented on more than one occasion that she looked better for it.

Maeve had put her head in her hands and when she moved them away Ida could see that she was fighting back tears. 'The girls miss their Aunt Ida. I miss my sister. We used to see you all the time and now I go weeks without even hearing from you.'

'Things change. I was single back then, I spent all of my free time with you guys and I enjoyed every second, but my life is with Cal now. I love him.'

Ida got the impression that Maeve had wanted to either laugh or roll her eyes but the restraint caused her to grimace and then smile weakly instead. 'Sometimes we can think we're in love when in fact we're...'

Ida interrupted. 'Maeve! Stop! Don't patronise me, okay?'

'I'm sorry. I just want what's best for you and... well, I don't know if Cal's it.'

'He is! Just because I'm not always available to babysit anymore doesn't mean I'm not happy.' Ida immediately regretted her words simply because she did not mean them, but the hurt on Maeve's face made her feel even worse. She knew that was not what Maeve was doing here, trying to talk her into babysitting Violet and Ivy. She could see the concern in her eyes and she knew it was genuine. She felt so torn. 'I'm sorry, I didn't mean that.'

There was an awkward silence before Maeve spoke again, all the things she'd wanted to say but now daren't crumbling before their eyes before she could move on – Ida knew what those things were just as much as Maeve did; they'd spoke about them before, many times.

'You haven't even been to visit Mum.' Her voice was low and neutral, devoid of the accusing tone Cal would later tell her was there along with the contempt in her eyes.

Ida lowered her gaze, unable to look at her.

'She doesn't have long left, Ida. I don't want you to miss out on saying goodbye.'

'I can't.'

'She's been asking for you.'

'I can't.' Ida stood, grabbing her bag from the back of her chair, and as she did her eyes caught a familiar car across the road – a truck with personalised plates. It was Cal's, and through the windscreen she could just make out his eyes. They were staring right at her.

'What? Of course I've been here! I didn't have a generator so I couldn't use most of the food.' She realised as she said it that she was tripping herself up; she'd told him the storm was recent and now here she was contradicting herself, failing to conceal her own lie. She didn't understand how Cal had been able to do it for so long, keeping up with the trail of deceit. How had he not tripped up over all the things he'd told her? Or had there been mistakes that she'd been blind to?

'Then what *have* you been eating?'

'I haven't had much of an appetite, Cal. I haven't been feeling myself.'

'You don't look like you've been starving yourself.'

They stood like that for what seemed an eternity to Ida, her lies set out for him to scrutinise and Cal deciding whether or not to dissect them further. For reasons Ida couldn't understand, he seemed to let it go.

'Let's get that drink.' He stepped to the side, allowing Ida to pass, but when she drew level with him he grabbed her arm, his fingers pressing into her flesh and spinning her round to face him. 'I might have saved you, Ida, but I can just as easily destroy you if you make me look like a fool.' He stormed into the house, letting the door shut behind him and leaving Ida stood outside, her eyes drifting back towards the hills.

CHAPTER THIRTY-FOUR

They sat and drank in silence, Ida's mind on Walker and what he'd told her. She felt guilty, as though she'd left him to deal with the fallout of opening up by himself, though she knew that would likely be what he wanted. She had spent so long in a certain mindset, equating the amount of things someone said to their level of devotion to her. Cal was all the things Walker was not: loud, emotional, jealous, commanding. They'd always had a fiery relationship, Ida and Cal, one minute it was passion and the next it was tears. Only now she realised how dangerous it was, all that fire, without the respite to let the flames fade away. It was wild and unpredictable, reckless and volatile. Ida knew that one day, if she wasn't careful, it would burn her to the ground.

'We should go and get the rest of the supplies.' Cal spoke as though nothing had happened, his tone casual, the anger from before now stored away in Ida's mind as another memory she wasn't sure she could recall accurately. It was the hardest thing about being with someone like Cal, she thought, the fact that he had caused her to doubt her own mind.

Ida nodded. She was drained, running on fumes that were

evaporating fast. She wanted to go to bed but she wasn't sure whether she'd be able to sleep with Cal here. She stood up and collected their empty mugs, placing them by the sink and looking out into the forest, beyond the river and the stepping stones. Everywhere reminded her of Walker and she hadn't realised just how much she'd begun to like that until now.

'Let's go.' Cal headed for the door, not pausing to wait for Ida which suited her just fine.

She caught up with him out in the field, the grass swaying around her hips and Cal lingering around a yellow gorse. 'I came out here looking for you earlier,' he said. Ida tried to continue walking but Cal reached out and took her by the wrist. 'I was worried. I didn't know where you'd gone.'

'I'm sorry, I didn't mean to worry you.'

'The thing is, while I was out here, I found something.' He bent down and reached towards the gorse, his hand in and out in a flash – mere seconds which allowed Ida to take a step back as she realised what it was he'd found. 'Why the fuck is my phone here, Ida?' He held it up to her, thrusting it towards her.

'I... I don't know,' she stuttered. 'Did you drop it?' She knew it was a mistake the moment she'd said it, accusing him of something they both knew hadn't happened. She knew Cal wouldn't tolerate it. His hand came at her without warning, the back of it meeting her cheek with a force that sent her sideways, her hands finding the ground as she fell. Her head was spinning. She closed her eyes for a moment, her hand clutching her cheek.

'Let's try again. Why the *fuck*...' he kicked her hard in the ribs, '...is my phone here?' She fell back onto the grass, the air thrust from her lungs. As she opened her eyes, her breathing fast and shallow, she saw him towering over her, blocking out the sun, its golden light casting him in silhouette. Ida squinted, trying to sit up, but he put his foot on her shoulder and pushed her back down with it.

'I took it,' she whispered, barely audible over the sound of her raspy breaths.

'Why?'

Her instinct was to lie – perhaps that's what happens when you've spent so long with someone like Cal, the deceit infecting everyone around them, seeping into her bones like a disease – but she knew it was futile. Sooner or later, she had to end this.

'Because I know you've been lying to me. I know the flu outbreak has been contained.'

Cal threw his head back and laughed to the sky, loud and maniacally. Ida sat up, watching him. Eventually he stopped and looked at her, his expression changing to one of disgust. It never failed to shock Ida, the way he could change in an instant, all warmth leaving him, just the cold hard shell of the man remaining.

'You ungrateful bitch.'

'Cal, I know! I've been into town, I've seen *people*.'

'Of course you did, not everyone's dead, Ida. Jesus Christ, you're stupid.'

'Don't say that. I'm not stupid. I've seen your phone. I unlocked it while you were sleeping. You have a wife! And a son for God's sake!'

Cal smiled, a big toothy grin that told her he was struggling to find the words. She didn't speak, she fought down the impulse to keep hurling accusations at him to give him time to respond. Eventually he shook his head. 'What are you talking about? You're mad.'

'No. No, I'm not. Don't call me mad.'

'I'm sorry, Ida, but you need to hear the truth. I've looked after you all this time, breaking my back to do my best for you, and this is how you repay me? How could I have a wife and child, Ida? I've spent all my time back and forth between London and the middle of fucking nowhere!'

'I saw pictures of your wedding, Cal!'

'What?'

'You and Verity. I know you got married. I saw the photos.'

'No, you saw old pictures of Verity and Ethan's wedding.'

'What? That doesn't even make sense!'

'They got married after your mum died. No one told you because you were too busy having a nervous fucking breakdown, making everything about yourself.'

Ida was shaking her head as though trying to stop his words entering her mind and polluting her thoughts. She knew he would do this; she knew he would try to twist it, but she hadn't been prepared for quite how he would do it.

'The boy... Otto...'

'Verity's nephew.'

'What? No. No, that's not right. I saw the messages between you.'

'What are you talking about, Ida? There are no messages between Verity and I. You've put two and two together and made five fucking thousand.'

'Don't do this, Cal. Don't try and turn things. I know what I saw! There's a whole town of people out there.' She threw her arm out and gestured towards the hills but as she did so she felt a sharp pain in her side catch her breath. She bent over, her hand clutching her ribs.

'And how did you get there? Eh, Ida? How did you get all the way into town?'

'That's not the point!'

'That's exactly the point. I'm out there getting you stocked up on wood, helping you like I always do, and where were you?'

She knew in her gut that Cal knew where she was. She wasn't sure whether he'd seen her or just worked it out, but he knew, and there was no point in fighting it.

'I was at Wa...' she began, but quickly stopped herself. 'I was at the man's house, the one with the dog that I told you about. I just went to give him something back that I'd borrowed.' Ida tried to stand, the pain in her side made it difficult but eventually she got to her feet, stepping back to put some distance between them. 'He helped me after the storm. The roof...' She looked up towards the tarp which Walker had put there and Cal followed her gaze.

'You let another man come here? To my house?'

'There was a hole in the roof!' Ida protested. 'The whole house flooded and the storms... they just kept coming. I didn't know what else to do!' The irony of Ida defending her actions while Cal hadn't even acknowledged his own was not lost on her, but this was the way things always went between them. Ida could feel herself being ground down by him already, questioning herself and what she'd seen.

'I can't believe you would do this to me, Ida. After everything I've done for you. Even in the middle of nowhere you manage to behave like a slut.' He shook his head at her, his eyes full of disgust. Ida could feel the old familiar thoughts surfacing: *What if I'm wrong? He* has *always looked out for me. He only does these things because he loves me.* She tried to push them away, focusing instead on the mountain of lies and the manipulation and control; the fact that she'd lost everyone she'd ever loved, all for a man who treated her with disdain, who made her feel worthless.

'Did you know about Maeve?' Ida asked him, not expecting to get an answer.

'She's dead,' he said flippantly. 'Didn't think you could handle the truth. See, that's what I do for you, Ida. I protect you. I know how delicate you are so I only tell you what you need to know.'

Ida wasn't listening. She couldn't. *She's dead.* Cal's words circled around in her head as though they were on a loop.

'Ida? Ida?' He was calling her name, his voice getting louder, commanding her attention. She looked at him, tears streaming down her face. Of course she already knew, she'd known since she'd seen the picture of her in the newspaper at Walker's; she'd grieved for her for weeks now but suddenly it felt as though she was finding out all over again, Cal confirming what she already knew to be true in such a cruel and brutal way. 'Does it feel good? Huh? Does it feel good to know what's going on out there? Or would you rather live in your little bubble, completely oblivious?'

'You don't get to decide that! You've lied to me! All this time, you've lied about why I'm here!'

Cal grabbed her shoulders, holding her in place, looking directly at her. 'You're here because you can't handle the real world, Ida. You're here for your own good. Your own *safety*! I did what I had to do.'

'Get your hands off me!' She shrugged her shoulders, pulling away from his grip and turning to leave. She needed to get away from him, to put some distance between them. She walked through the gate, towards the river and the forest, but before she reached the edge Cal's hand was in her hair, his fingers gripping at the roots and pulling her head back hard.

'You don't walk away from me!' He'd turned her to face him, his hand still entwined in her hair, his face almost touching hers. He was talking through clenched teeth, saliva showering her skin. She closed her eyes for a moment, hoping that when she opened them again it would all be a dream, that she could start again and next time get it right. She realised now that this wasn't what she needed, there was no good way for this to end and not all things needed wrapping up before they could be cast to one side. She should have disappeared without a trace leaving Cal with the weight of the unknown.

Ida put her hand over Cal's and tried to counter his pulling by pushing. Her head was sore and her neck was aching from the position he was holding her in. 'Let go of me!' she shouted.

'I told you not to make a fool out of me, Ida.' His other hand reached for her throat, his fingers wrapping around it. 'You should have listened!' He dropped her to the ground and sat straddling her waist, both hands now encircling her throat. She tried to speak but she couldn't, the pressure was too much. She couldn't breathe. She tried hitting out at him with her hands but she could hardly reach him. Instead, her fingers found the roots of the grass, the bristly leaves and the dry earth. Then, somewhere among it all, her fingers found something hard and jagged. A rock.

She gripped it in her right hand and moved it closer to her, careful not to let him see what she was doing. Cal's face was red with rage, his hands still gripped tightly around her throat. She could feel her life being extinguished, her eyes bulging and the blood in her head pulsating loudly in her ears.

He was hunched over, his face leaning closer to her as he held her in place, watching what he was doing to her. A long string of saliva fell from his mouth as he grimaced, straining to apply more pressure. She took the rock and slammed it as hard as she could into his temple.

His hands were off her neck, shooting up to his head as he called out in pain. Ida gulped desperately for air, her throat dry and bruised and her neck stiff and painful. Cal had lost concentration momentarily; he looked dazed. Ida wriggled out from under him and got to her feet, her side throbbing along with her neck. She couldn't get enough air, her breathing erratic. Her heart was racing and her hands shaking.

Cal tried to get to his feet, slowly and unsteadily, one of his hands pushing against the ground as the other held on to his head. Ida could see a thin trickle of blood running down the side of his head and disappearing into his beard. She watched him stagger around, backing away from him; they were both in shock, adrenaline pumping through their bodies as they grappled with what to do next. Cal's eyes found Ida as she stood trembling.

'You... you fucking bitch...' He moved towards her but Ida could see he was unstable, his eyes struggling to focus. Her instinct was to run but she fought it, quickly burying it under all the anger.

Instead, she ran at him, wild and screaming, her hands stretched out in front of her. They connected with Cal's chest as he struggled to comprehend what was happening. She saw his confused eyes flicker, widening in shock as he realised he was falling. Ida watched as he rolled awkwardly down the riverbank, his head connecting with the first stepping stone, his arm flailing limply into the water which ran there.

She stood at the edge, motionless, just like Cal.

CHAPTER THIRTY-FIVE

C al didn't move and Ida couldn't bring herself to go down to the river to check on him. She sat on the bank, battered and bruised, allowing herself a moment of quiet. She felt numb, as though she were drifting above the world in a dreamlike state without being able to anchor herself to anything.

The moment stretched out into a period of time Ida could not account for. She'd slipped into a state of shock where her memories drifted unhindered by her mind. She saw her mother, young and healthy, her red hair loose and untamed. She smiled at Ida but didn't speak. In her mind's eye, Ida counted the freckles on her nose and examined the green of her eyes; all the things she hadn't stopped to notice while she was alive; all the things she hadn't stopped to appreciate about the woman who'd been taken from her when she needed her the most.

Then she saw Maeve, sweet, kind Maeve, a mirror image of their mother, tall and graceful, her porcelain skin contrasting with the red of her hair. She was playing with her girls, running around their garden smiling and laughing, Violet and Ivy giving chase and tumbling over their own feet. Ida wanted to reach out and touch them, to scoop them up and hold them close. Her heart ached for them.

As the temperature cooled and the sun travelled west, Ida felt something cold touch her cheek. She turned to see Chief nuzzling at her, his nose sniffing at her face. Walker was just behind him, his stick in his hand and concern in his eyes. She looked at him, then she looked down the bank at Cal. Walker followed her gaze, seeing what she saw, but there was no judgement on his face, no wild alarm or look of horror. Instead, he put the stick on the ground beside him and made his way down the uneven hill, watching his step until he came to the river and the unmoving body that lay partially submerged in it. Walker kneeled beside him and held two fingers to Cal's neck, checking for life Ida wasn't sure was there. She could see him examining the wound on Cal's temple, then the back of his head where he'd hit the stepping stone he now lay next to. After a minute or so, Walker rose and looked up to Ida.

'He's alive.'

Ida felt relieved. She hated Cal – she really, truly hated him – but she wasn't a killer and she didn't want that on her conscience if only for selfish reasons: she knew that she would struggle under the weight of it, that it would impact the rest of her life and tie her endlessly to the man who had brought her such pain. She didn't want that burden.

Walker made his way back up the hill to Ida and sat next to her, crossing one leg over the other in front of him. 'He'll wake up at some point – maybe in a few minutes, maybe not until tomorrow, but he'll wake up. So if you have stuff you've got to do before then... we need to do it now.'

Ida turned to face him. 'You can't get involved. You should go, pretend you never saw anything.'

'We both know I'm not going anywhere.'

'I can't ask you to help me with this... I got myself into this mess.'

'You didn't ask me to help you and you didn't get yourself into this mess. He did.' He nodded his head towards Cal who lay motionless on the ground, his arm moving gently in the current of the water.

Ida couldn't think straight. She didn't want Walker to have to swoop in and save her again, she wanted to think and act for herself, to make a plan and – if Walker insisted on helping – to tell him what she needed him to do. She lay back on the ground, wincing at the pain in her side, and stared up at the sky.

She felt Walker's eyes on her, taking in the red ring around her throat and the bruising on her cheek. He didn't ask her about them, he didn't need to, he simply sat by her side and kept watch while she sorted through her chaotic mind, trying to make sense of things she probably never would. She took some deep breaths and thought of her sister – what would Maeve tell her to do? She remembered the things she had told Walker about her: *She'd say we had to keep our fire burning so we could do anything we wanted in life, because no one messes with fire.*

After a while, she sat up and looked at Walker. 'I know what I need to do.'

The smoke billowed from the house, thick grey plumes which disappeared into the darkening skies. She'd used the petrol to start it, pouring it over the place she'd once called home, splashing it over everything which had once given her comfort – the books and the jigsaws, the photos and the letters. Walker had asked her if she was sure she didn't want to save anything but she'd shook her head and told him no. She didn't want anything that would remind her of Cal, she knew she would carry enough of him with her without the material things to exacerbate the pain.

She'd lit the match herself and threw it from the doorway. Walker and Chief stood far enough away to give her the sense that this was all her own doing, while being close enough to know she wasn't alone.

Walker had taken Cal's phone and keys from his pockets and handed them to Ida, unlocked and ready to use. They'd walked to Cal's truck where the signal was sketchy but useable, then she'd used the phone to record a video of herself, the personalised number plate of his truck in the background. She'd sent it to Verity, telling her about all the abuse she'd endured, the control and manipulation, knowing that it would resonate with her. She didn't know whether it would be enough to free her – and their son – but she had to try.

She'd left the truck unlocked with the phone and keys inside, then she'd headed back to Walker's place with him, Chief leading the way. Walker had used the binoculars to keep an eye on the dirt path, looking for any movement in the truck. Ida had sat on one of the chairs outside, a blanket draped over her shoulders and their dinner cooking on the firepit. She wasn't hungry but she'd found some degree of comfort in the normalcy of preparing a meal. A couple of hours after she'd sent the house up in smoke, Walker turned to her.

'He's gone.'

She felt as though she'd been holding her breath without realising. 'You can see? He's definitely gone?'

'I watched him drive away. He's gone.' He sat down beside her.

'Do you think he'll come looking for me?'

'I think he's in a rush to get home.'

'But after that... I might have ruined his marriage.'

Walker thought about it for a while and Ida could tell he

didn't want to lie, but nor did he want to scare her. 'Men like him... they don't stop.'

Ida knew it was true, but hearing Walker say it still made her chest ache. She swallowed hard against the dryness of her throat. 'I know.'

They sat like that for some time, neither of them needing to talk. Ida was thinking, trying to organise the confusion in her mind into some sort of order. She needed a plan beyond that moment; something to guide her. Something to hold on to.

'I think he saw me coming to yours earlier.' She regretted not telling him this sooner. In all the chaos she'd forgot to mention something which could have put him in danger. 'I'm sorry.'

Walker shrugged. 'I've lived in the wild for long enough to know a thing or two about protecting myself. Besides, I don't need to stay here forever.'

'But it's your home.'

'It's a pile of wood and nails that I built myself. I can start again.'

Ida wanted to reach out and hold him, to throw her arms around him and never let him go. Instead, she settled for taking his hand in hers. They sat like that for a while, listening to the river and the birds, a mountain of possibilities between them.

'I came to tell you something earlier, when I found you on the bank.' Ida turned to look at him. 'My name... it's Jack.'

Ida smiled, tears stinging her eyes. She knew what it had taken for him to tell her that, to share this part of himself that he had shielded for so long.

'Jack,' Ida said, mulling the name over, trying to decide whether it suited him. He was Walker to her, and she thought that he always would be. 'I think there are some things that I need to do.'

'I had a feeling there would be.'

'I don't know how to thank you for everything you've done for me.'

Walker didn't respond at first, he just sat watching the fire, his legs outstretched in front of him. After a while, he cleared his throat. 'Maybe after you've done what you need to do, you can find me.'

'I'm afraid I won't be able to.'

'I'll be here.'

'But what about Cal?'

'We can cross that bridge if you come back.'

Ida pulled her knees up to her chest, her hand still holding Walker's. She felt the warmth of the fire in front of her, the flames flickering, the smell of the cooking food wafting in the breeze. She felt a peace which defied the situation; a solace which told her that she wouldn't be gone for long. She knew it wasn't going to be easy, leaving this all behind, if only for a moment in time. Her mind drifted to her nieces and she wondered whether they would remember her.

'*When* I come back,' she said. 'I still haven't read that book.' Walker looked at her and frowned. '*The Quiet Space Between Us*,' she clarified.

'I'll save it for you.'

Ida smiled and let go of Walker's hand, her arms encircling her legs. Walker got up to tend to the food and Ida tilted her head back to look at the sky. The stars were starting to appear, little specks of light among the darkness.

Ida watched them, focusing all her attention on the light.

THE END

ACKNOWLEDGEMENTS

I am incredibly fortunate to have so many wonderful people supporting me. This list is by no means an exhaustive one, so to anyone and everyone who has helped me along the way – thank you!

To the team at Bloodhound Books – Betsy, Fred, Tara, Hannah and Shirley – thank you for your continued support and guidance. Special thanks to my editor, Ian, for your patience and insight, and for helping to shape Ida's story.

As always, I am indebted to my first readers – Nicki, Abby, Beth, Caron and Adrian. Thank you for taking the time to read my work in its early form and provide some much needed feedback.

Thank you to the Debut 22 group for being so wonderful and supportive.

To my mum, dad and parents-in-law – thank you for always being there to offer practical support so I can write.

Thank you to my children: I do hope that one day, in the future, you can enjoy my books and know that your love and enthusiasm helped shape them.

To my husband – thank you for your love and encouragement, and for always having my back.

And last but not least – thank *you*, the reader. This story has such a special place in my heart. I hope that you enjoyed reading it as much as I enjoyed writing it.